A NEW BEGINNING

THE WHITE CHRONICLES, BOOK ONE

J. E. THOMPSON

ARC BOOK CLUB, LLC

Cover by Jake @ J Caleb Design

ISBN: 978-1-952677-01-4 (Paperback)

ISBN: 978-1-952677-00-7 (eBook)

ISBN: 978-1-952677-02-1 (Audiobook)

For my wife and best friend, Wallis.

1

VEXX WHITE

Vexx felt a lump in his throat as he avoided a deep rut in the dirt road. It had been quite some time since he'd last left Cloudbury, and he couldn't help but reflect on the occasion. He'd stood tall back then, as tall as any twelve-year-old could have, anyway, no doubt looking as proud and arrogant and ambitious as he knew he'd been. As he still was, for that matter, even if his dreams had all been reduced to dust.

They were fools to expel me. Fools! Besides, the best necromancy requires only the freshest of corpses. What kind of magical academy is built next to a cemetery but also forbids black magic? That's practically entrapment.

His hands fumbled at his sides, his pale skin a stark contrast against his black apprentice's robes. After a moment, they settled uncomfortably into his pockets. They'd left him the clothes on his back, at least, even though they'd taken everything else. He had a few coppers in there, along with a finger bone the administrators hadn't noticed, but he doubted any of that would get him more than the simplest of meals.

Still, Dred Wyrm started with less, and look at him now! The most renowned dungeoneer there is.

Vexx came to an uncertain halt, suddenly realizing that he had walked through all of Cloudbury, his hometown now strange to him. Still, there was no mistaking the house where he'd grown up. The way the grass grew wild, the way the straw ceiling sloped, the gaps in the...windows...

Vexx squinted. *Hang on. What's happened to it?*

Without thinking, he burst forward, leaping up the slope and up to the ancient wooden door. He put his hand on the bronze handle and pushed it open, ducking his head to fold his lanky frame through the doorway.

"Father, I have re-" he trailed off, taking in the cobwebs in the corners, the dusty table with a few letters on it. He numbly walked over, glancing into the corners, but there was no sign of life. Vexx's heart was already sinking. His father would not have let the house fall into this state of disrepair. Not that cantankerous old coot. No, not the old man who had Vexx scrubbing all day and all night any time it looked like he'd tracked in a few stray specks of mud.

Vexx rummaged through the scrolls sitting on the table, opening a few at random, quickly scanning through them. Messages from the town council, something about non-payment of taxes, a death certificate...

Vexx's vision blurred as he stared at the words. Adelius White, dead of exposure following the late storms. *Surely someone would have sent a message to the Magical Academy at Fallanden...*he blinked away the unexpected moisture in his eyes.

Eventually, he managed to wade through the paperwork, his surprise fading to grim resignation. From what he could piece together, following his father's death, the house had been taken for non-payment of taxes and subsequently sold. And clutched in his hands was the one scroll that bore Vexx White's own name.

"To the heir of the Adelius White estate, Vexx White, is due a share of the house's proceeds. If the heir presents this scroll at the town council building on 14 Marionberry Lane, Cloudbury, he or she will receive—"

Vexx folded it up before looking at the sum and stuffed it in his apprentice robe's voluminous pocket. Somehow, he didn't feel like spending another minute in this place.

"Well," Vexx said in the dismal silence, rising from his chair. "No time like the present."

Vexx dusted himself off and strode purposefully towards the door. He left without a backward glance.

2

THE PROCEEDS

Like most towns in Ilor, the economy of Cloudbury depended on the large forest growing around the Lifeless Hills. Vexx passed a band of foresters trudging along the street, large axes resting on their shoulders. A few men in their early twenties looked his way in idle curiosity and Vexx stared back despite himself, wondering if he could recognize any of them from his childhood. They were about the same age, after all, though he'd been saved from that fate by admittance to the Fallanden Magical Academy.

Or so I thought. What's there for me now?

The council building wasn't far away, a rickety old building that slumped to the side as if it had been shoved off its foundation by a group of trolls. It bore the grime and half-rotted wood that was standard for older buildings in Cloudbury. The town was a sad, provincial place, which was a fact that Vexx White had never quite realized until he'd left to attend the Academy in the bustling city of Fallanden.

It wasn't as though he'd travelled much, of course.

He'd been all but confined behind the academy's walls. And then, when he had been expelled, Vexx hadn't had any reason to go anywhere else but home.

And now, there wasn't even a home for him anymore.

Vexx pressed open the rickety door and stood uncertainly in the dim interior. A white-haired woman handed over a sheaf of documents to a well-dressed man at a counter.

"Next," she said, as the man left with his bundle of documents. Vexx scanned the empty room, and after a moment, he approached the clerk.

"Um, Vexx White. I understand my father Adelius White had his house seized after he passed away."

"Oh yes," the woman said, squinting up at him. "You must be the son. I knew Adelius, actually."

"Oh? How was the funeral?"

"I didn't go," she replied, sliding out a drawer in her ancient wooden desk. "Adelius was a bastard, and I was glad to see him dead. Now, here we are." She unfurled the scroll on her desk, then tossed a small sack of coins beside it. "Your share of the proceeds. You attended the Magical Academy, correct? Then I take it you can spell," she said, tapping an inkwell on her desk.

Vexx smiled. "I know all sorts of spells."

She shot him an exasperated look.

"Ah, and I know how to spell," he added, picking up the quill resting beside the inkwell.

"You have your father's sense of humor. Just sign here, here, and here."

Vexx scribbled away, then finally set the quill down. "What now?"

"Now?" The clerk slid the coins over to him. "That's for you to decide, young man. But your father's former house is now the property of the town council. Keep out of it." She paused, her expression softening almost imperceptibly. "If you're looking for work, some of the farmers could use a hand. Perhaps a logging company will take you on as an apprentice." She shrugged.

Vexx grimaced before nodding silently and scooping up the small bag of coins. His mind was a whirl of confused emotions.

What should I do now?

3

VEXX AND KAYLIN

He stood uncertainly before the small grave marked with the simple carved words: Adelius White, Devoted Husband and Father. Vexx glanced left and right.

A short chat wouldn't hurt, would it? But it isn't as though I've mastered the art of necromancy. Vexx's hand raised a hair and he stood there, motionless. He shook his head and tucked his hand into his pocket.

"Rest in peace, Dad. Maybe we'll talk later."

The cemetery was a silent, peaceful place, and the orchard beside it blocked out the hustle and bustle of nearby Cloudbury. Vexx inhaled the pleasant aroma of the apple trees as he turned away from his father's grave. He stared ahead, past the fence that encircled the cemetery. He had vaulted a fence very much like it several times before, paying midnight visits to a different cemetery, practicing the forbidden Black Arts.

Vexx grimaced. *And then I'd been expelled.* It wasn't a pleasant thought, and he cast it aside as he strode outward into Cloudbury, uncertain of his exact destination. *I've spent too much time in the past. It's time I made a new future for myself.*

He strode past a couple horsemen, perhaps on patrol along the periphery of the Lifeless Hills, a region he remembered to be quite dangerous. Vexx nodded at a family of farmers, who greeted him politely in return, likely returning to their farmstead after selling their wares at the town market. *I always thought I'd be a mage, but now, I'm worse off than even those farmers. What am I supposed to do now? I thought my father could at least give me some advice or provide me with lodging while I figured things out, but...*

Vexx grumbled to himself as he strode down the dirt road that bisected Cloudbury. *First, they kick me out of the academy, and now this?* He rummaged through the sack, feeling the varying weights of metal pieces within. A paltry sum, but more than enough to get him well and truly drunk. *It's been ages since I've been back. Where should I go?*

A blacksmith paused between heavy blows on the forge and glanced over.

"Excuse me, stranger, but where's the nearest bar?"

"Just down the road," the bare-chested man said, gesturing with a pair of tongs. He squinted at Vexx. "Wait, aren't you that White boy?"

Vexx grimaced. "Thanks for the directions," he muttered, quickening his pace. He could see the bar now: a low, squat structure of timber with a wide, rickety door. Beside it swung a bulletin board on a stand, currently empty of bounties. He pushed his way inside and was almost overwhelmed by the clamoring of drunk patrons from within.

Bottles clanked as adventurers celebrated their earnings for the day, their raucous laughter and the cloying stench of dungeon rot told Vexx everything he needed to know about them. At the table beside them, an orc was furiously playing five finger fillet on his own, enthusiastically plunging the stained blade of a small knife into the splintered top of the table.

Vexx strolled past an unconscious sorcerer to where a young elf woman was pleading with the unimpressed barkeep.

"Just one quest," she said, leaning close. The candlelight danced over her tanned skin, the elf's skimpy armor leaving very little to the imagination.

Vexx couldn't help but give her an appreciative once over as he sidled closer to the bar. *Not so bad for an elf. Light on armor for an adventurer, though.*

The barkeep shook his head as he polished a mug. "I don't know if you're up to it...Kaylin, did you say your name was? That shortbow there seems pretty shoddy. Do you know how to use it?"

"Do I?"

The elf perked up and reached for the shortbow strapped to her back, but in her haste, the end of her bow caught on the stool beside her and she stumbled back. She turned and tripped, crashing unceremoniously into Vexx's arms. He stood there for a moment with his arms draped awkwardly around her, watching as a pretty blush suffused her cheeks.

"Um...hello."

Vexx smiled despite himself. "Hello."

A clang broke the uncomfortable silence as the barkeep set the clean mug down. "Oh, I didn't realize you two were together," the barkeep said. Kaylin began to stammer a denial, but by some impulse, Vexx's hand shot out and covered her mouth.

"That's right," he said with a smile. "Vexx White, dungeoneer for hire."

"Well, I do have a two person job," the barkeep said thoughtfully as Vexx released the elf woman, who scowled in silence as she got to her feet. "But I doubt you'll like it." He tilted his head. "Ya ever tangled with goblins?"

4

DUNGEONEERS

Vexx's heart pounded, and it wasn't just from being next to the attractive elf, who was now brushing her flaxen hair aside and muttering something unintelligible.

Of course, why didn't I think about it before? I could become a dungeoneer for real, just like Dred Wyrm! I have nothing keeping me from it anymore, and I could use the money. Besides...I've learned a few tricks over the years.

Vexx snapped his fingers, a puff of flame hovering in place above his outstretched palm. "Goblins? Goblins are easy," Vexx said with a derisive snort. He hadn't fought goblins before. Truth be told, he'd only seen them once or twice, but they didn't seem like they'd be much trouble. Vexx had trained hard at the academy, excelling in the darker arts since he was 'a bit too much of a natural talent,' as he had heard his teachers mutter amongst themselves.

"Well, it's really only one goblin," the barkeep said slowly. "But he's a quick little bastard."

Vexx frowned. "You know him?"

"We're not exactly on friendly terms. He's been killing my sheep. I spotted him finally, leaving my farm for a dugout. I figure the two of you could flush him out," he said, glancing back at the elf. "Think you can handle that, missy?"

"Of course!" she exclaimed with a broad smile, her green eyes glimmering in the glow of the tavern's candles. "My name's Kaylin Lulynn, and I was the best shot in my village! We'll do it, no problem," she said happily as she turned to look at Vexx, nearly knocking the mug out of the barkeep's hands. "Hey, do you think—"

But Vexx was already frowning, the excitement draining away. "One goblin? You've got to be kidding me. That's far below my—"

The elf tugged on his sleeve and gave him a pleading look. "Don't say that, Vexx! Sure, it'll be easy, but…do it for me? Will you?"

"Uh…yeah, sure," Vexx stammered, and the elf let go with a smile.

The barkeeper frowned at them, smoothing down his salt and pepper mustache. "I'm really not sure about you two. You," he said, pointing an accusing mug at Vexx, "are wearing the most peculiar pajamas I've ever seen. And you," he continued, ignoring Vexx's protests about Academy Initiate clothing, "must be the clumsiest elf I've ever met. I thought you elves were supposed to be nimble and graceful or something."

"Eheh, well…I'm very lucky…" Kaylin stammered, looking down. She sniffed. "Decently charismatic," she added, wiping away a tear.

He gave her another dubious look and shook his head. "Listen, I don't think the two of you are up for the job. Hell, you can barely stay on your feet, elf girl. I'm not going to send you to your deaths."

Vexx felt a surge of sympathy well up in him and he

approached the bar. He pulled out his coin purse and slammed it on the counter. "There's ten silver pieces in there, old man. In two days, we will come back with proof that we've killed the goblin, and we'll take fifteen pieces in return. If we don't make it back, then it won't make a difference to you. What do you say?"

"Old man, am I?" the barkeep muttered, clasping a hairy hand around the coin purse. "The name's Pollander. You know, you could learn a thing or two about charisma from your friend here, boy. Still, it's an acceptable enough deal. Bring me the fiend's ear and I'll get you your fifteen pieces. And, why not, I'll sweeten it up with a mug of ale for you both." Pollander took the coin purse along with him, moving behind the bar. "Might be the last ones you get," he muttered, just barely audible over the controlled chaos of the tavern interior.

"Oh…oh, I don't drink," Kaylin said, as Vexx took a seat at the bar. He raised his eyebrows.

"Really? Why's that?"

"I just get too carried away," she said. "Trust me, it's not good."

Vexx grunted. "Two for me, then. I'll need all I can get, with all the shit I've been through lately. And one lousy goblin…"

The mugs slid over and the barkeep moved farther down the counter, shouting at a group of barbarians who were howling with laughter at one joke or another. Kaylin gingerly slid her ale across to Vexx, who was downing his eagerly. He slammed his mug down, wiping the froth from his lips.

"So, what have you been through?" Kaylin asked. "I should get to know my new healer sidekick, after all."

"Healer?" Vexx frowned, and then a second later, blanched in horror. "*Sidekick?*"

"Yes, well…you said Vexx White after all. And your robes? You must be some sort of apprentice healer."

"This again? I'm a healer because my last name is White? That's borderline racist, you know."

"It's not a *human* thing," she said. "It's because you're, uh…well, you have robes on."

"And you have…" Vexx trailed off as he glanced over. Kaylin was clad in tight leather armor, and not much of it. Her bow was strapped along her back and a knife rested in her belt, but her long, shapely legs bore no protection whatsoever. He glanced away after a second. "Not a lot on," he finished lamely.

"Well, I'm just starting out," she huffed. "And I want this mission to go right. There's still plenty of daylight left. Will you be able to back me up after those ales, Vexx?"

"Get this straight, elf. I'm no healer, and I'm nobody's sidekick," Vexx said, slamming his empty mug on the counter and picking up the second one.

"Mmm," Kaylin answered noncommittally.

5

GOBLIN HUNTING

"One goblin," Vexx muttered as they walked down the road. "Talk about small stakes. I'll never be a renowned dungeoneer like Dred Wyrm by doing little jobs like this. What I really need to do is go big."

"Who's Dred Wyrm?" Kaylin asked, her strides hurried as she tried to keep pace with him. She had her bow out and strummed the taut bowstring, nodding to herself in satisfaction.

Vexx raised his eyebrows in surprise. "What, did you grow up under a rock?"

"No, just in a forest. It's only been a few days since I've left to seek my fortune."

"Well, he's only the most legendary dungeoneer around. Dragonborn, and he never fails a quest. They say he won an arm wrestling contest with an ogre, a drinking contest against a dwarf, and then a battle of wits against an arch sorcerer—and that was after the drinking! He's the strongest, toughest, and smartest person there is."

"Really…"

"Really," Vexx said firmly before stumbling over a rock

in the road. He gathered himself up with ruffled dignity. Those ales had hit him a little harder than he had expected. He patted his stomach. He could use something to eat...

"The barkeep said it was just to the left, right?" Kaylin asked as she took the left fork in the road just outside Cloudbury.

"I believe so..." Vexx replied. "I wasn't really listening."

"Two hundred paces, I think he said. Ah, that farmhouse just to the right. He didn't mention the fire, though."

Vexx blinked and the two continued strolling up in silence. The farmhouse was fine, but not far away, a barn was set ablaze. They watched as smoke rose into the sky, the reddish orange of the flames merged with the setting sun just behind the mountains.

"No...he did not."

"Is..." Kaylin leaned forward, staring intently. Then she turned to Vexx with a smile. "That's our goblin! Just there, to the right of the burning barn?"

"Really?" Vexx squinted. "I can't see that far."

"Oh, that's right," she said, already nocking an arrow to her bowstring, "the elders always said you humans were astoundingly shortsighted." She pulled it back to her long ear, breathing out slightly, and then the bowstring twanged as the arrow sped off.

In the distance, Vexx saw a small shape moving to the side.

"Agh, I missed it! Vexx, do you think you can—"

"I'm on it," Vexx said, already sprinting ahead, his boots splashing as he ran through the mud of the farm.

The barn was just up ahead, and he snapped his fingers, a spark bursting into life at the tip of his pointer finger.

No point in worrying about starting fires at this point.

He saw the shape bolt out from behind the barn; a squat figure clad in hides. *A goblin.*

Vexx slowed, whipping his right hand up, firing a firebolt and then following it up with another. The first burst on the goblin's left shoulder and it shrieked as it staggered to the side, the second firebolt just barely missed and landed in the mud behind it, smoldering away. An instant later an arrow sprouted from the goblin's chest and it fell to the ground.

"I got it!" Kaylin squealed as she ran up.

Vexx frowned. "No, I got it."

Kaylin peered over. "Never mind that. We got his goblin problem sorted. Vexx, do you think you can put that fire out?"

He grimaced as he looked over. "You know, I…kind of specialized in fire magic. But…" he concentrated, and then ice grew around his fist. "I'll see what I can do," he grunted, already tiring from the effort, as he fired a concentrated burst of ice at the barn. The flames licking the side puttered and then faded away as he steadied his aim.

"Uh, Vexx?"

"Yeah?" he said, straining as he blasted the barn with cooling, icy winds. "Kinda busy here!"

"So, uh…the barkeep said 'goblin,' right? Not 'goblins'?"

Vexx gritted his teeth, moving over from a charred window to the doorframe, the burning fire already receding. "Yeah. He said just one goblin."

"Well, it's just that. Uh. There are…a lot of goblins around."

With a final burst of effort, Vexx extinguished the last of the flames and whirled around. "I don't see any…oh."

A half-dozen goblins in an assortment of rough hides and furs glared at them, their beady little eyes glowing red in the fading light, and the one at the head of the pack pointed a jagged scimitar at the two of them. Vexx licked his lips before glancing at Kaylin, who was nervously nocking another arrow onto her bowstring.

Distantly, the old warnings came to him. *Dungeoneering was no way to make a living. For every Dred Wyrm, there were a thousand corpses rotting in a cave some-where. Most dungeoneers don't even make it past their first couple adventures…*

Vexx felt the exhaustion in his body as he sidestepped close to Kaylin. She stood there beside him, arrow nocked and readied, her arm twitching with the tension.

"You and me," Vexx said, despite the fear. "Together. We got this."

Kaylin made a small sound. And then, with a chorus of menacing bellows, the goblins charged forward.

6

CHARGE

Shoving his fear aside, Vexx raised both his hands, frigid mist drifted out of his left hand as fire burst from his right. He fired left and right, bolts of ice and fire crashing into the charging line of goblins, the closest brandishing a spear before it stumbled when Kaylin's shot buried itself in the goblin's leg. An axe whirled at Vexx and he took two steps backward, throwing his head back as the axe head swung past. Vexx grasped the haft of the axe and sent a surge of fire magic outward, charring and burning it until the axe head fell to the ground.

The goblin blinked, its eyes boggling in confusion, and Vexx fired flames into it at close range. The goblin squealed as it fell to the ground and Vexx turned, his eyes wild. Most of the goblins were downed, but two others were hemming Kaylin in, the elf desperately parrying a scimitar with her knife. She screamed as another goblin raked her side with its jagged spear.

Vexx surged forward, his exhaustion forgotten, firing firebolt after firebolt into the spear-wielding goblin, who staggered to the side before finally falling. Kaylin slashed the other goblin, and Vexx's last fireball put an end to the fight.

Kaylin and Vexx stood there for a moment, panting in exhaustion, glancing at each other as they recovered in the eerie silence.

"You alright?"

"I…" Kaylin took an unsteady step forward and collapsed onto the dirt. The elf took labored breaths in and out. "Agh…that last one really got me. Can you take a look?"

Vexx glanced over. A few of the straps were ripped, a reddish line traced her side, and a small trail of blood trickled down from the spear cut. "It's not that bad. I have a bandage in my pack," he said, reaching back and rummaging through his satchel.

"You really can't heal, can you?" she gritted out, teeth clenched and eyes squeezed shut.

"No," Vexx said, tying the bandage tight. "Look, I'll buy you a healing draught when we get back, alright? Can you walk?"

"May…maybe."

He shook his head, hefted Kaylin up and held his arm behind her. "With me, let's go. I know a place where we can stay, it's not very far away."

The elf clenched her teeth and threw an arm around Vexx. Together, they began walking away at a slow, steady pace.

"I was clumsy," she said after a while. "Too clumsy."

"Hey, we got them in the end," Vexx replied with a reassuring pat on her shoulder. "You weren't half bad, you know."

"Yeah, you too," Kaylin said, the silence lingering as

they made their way down the quiet road. "So, you're from here?"

"Kind of…I grew up just down the road. It was my parent's house, but my mom died some time ago. And my dad…well, he died recently. But anyway. We can hole up there tonight, but that'll be it. No, I think I'll be hitting the road from here on out."

"Ah," Kaylin said. "I did that myself, not too long ago. I thought it would go easier. But…still alive, right? Still alive."

PARTNERS

Morning came, the old house chilly and damp as Vexx came to his feet. He groaned, still feeling the exhaustion of his depleted magical energies. Vexx looked around and couldn't stop himself from reminiscing about half-remembered routines in his father's old house. It felt bizarre to be back after all those years. And especially bizarre knowing he was no longer welcome here.

As Vexx readied himself, he periodically glanced outside the windows. There could be guards from town coming, as far as he knew, or perhaps prospective buyers. He'd placed Kaylin in a different bedroom to rest over the night and now hesitated at the door of the guest room.

Finally, he rapped his knuckles against it twice. The door creaked open after a few moments and Kaylin smiled at him. Her leather armor was resting on a chair, her skintight underclothes leaving little to the imagination.

"Good morning, Vexx! How did you sleep?"

"Ah...well," he said, mustering all the willpower he could to avert his eyes. "And you?"

"Oh, just fine! I'm just cleaning up now," Kaylin

responded, her voice cheery as ever. "These human houses are something else! Nothing like a treehouse."

Vexx grunted. "Well, we need to leave soon. There's no coming back here."

"Don't worry yourself, Vexxy, I'm just about ready."

Vexx frowned. *Vexxy? Still, at least she seems to be doing fine. The cut didn't look bad, but sometimes weapons can have poison effects.* "How are you feeling?" Vexx asked.

"Much better," she said with a half-convincing smile. "I'm ready for the next one, partner. Did you turn in the bounty?"

"Partner?" Vexx asked with a sniff. "That's assuming a lot," he muttered. Still, it was a good deal better than 'side-kick,' and they had fought together well enough. *I suppose even Dred Wyrm fights in a party from time to time.*

Kaylin shrugged and padded over to the adjoining washroom.

"No, I was waiting for you," Vexx said, examining a fresh tear in his apprentice robes. *If business picks up, I'll have to upgrade my look.* "I don't think he'll be too pleased about the damage to his barn."

The splash of a wash basin was his only response. Vexx turned away, walking to the main window and looking out. It was a fine view, the tops of trees visible in the distance, his father's house secluded some distance away from Cloudbury. *I doubt I'll be returning, though. One way or another, I'll have to earn room and board.*

A hand grasped his arm and he jerked away in shock. "Let's go!" Kaylin said, tugging him forward before letting go, already pushing the door open. "I want that bounty turned in."

36 HOURS

"You know what I saw last night, *dungeoneers*?" Pollander asked in a profoundly disappointed tone as they approached the counter.

Vexx and Kaylin exchanged glances. This wasn't going as expected. Vexx cleared his throat.

"The barn was already—"

"Another dead sheep. And, oh yes, I heard Farmer Henderson's barn burned down over the evening. He was very puzzled to find a band of dead goblins in his fields." The barkeeper inclined his head. "Was that your doing? You didn't burn his barn, did you?" he asked with a glare. "You're no fire magician, right?"

"Me? No," Vexx said with a laugh. "I'm just a simple healer. That was all the goblins."

"Ah…so it was you two! What were you doing over there?"

"Got a bit…turned around, is all," Vexx said with a weak smile.

"Like I said, follow Tower Road past the end of Cloudbury, straight to the farms just below the Lifeless

Hills. Then, just to the right on Alabaster Avenue, the location is three houses down."

"I knew it was to the right," Kaylin said, tapping her finger on her cheek thoughtfully.

"I don't recall you mentioning it," Vexx said with a grimace. "Damn. Any chance of a reward for killing those goblins?"

The barkeeper snorted. "Henderson had a quest listed, as it happens, but I would never have given it to you two. So no rewards, besides the loot you left behind."

"What loot?" Vexx and Kaylin asked together.

The barkeep grinned as he checked off the bounty. "Word to the wise, my new dungeoneers," he said, moving across the bar counter to refill a mug. "Go over the bodies later. A bit of loot like that can make you more than a bit of profit."

Vexx groaned. "So all that was for nothing?"

"Gave you a bit of experience, didn't it?" the barkeeper asked, moving back over to them. "Anyway, the job's still on. Just one goblin, and the blood trail is still fresh. You have 36 hours, dungeoneers, and I suggest you hurry."

Vexx and Kaylin exchanged pained glances. "Fine," Vexx muttered, and the two of them made their way back to the door. "Damn it all," Vexx muttered to himself as they stepped back out into the shining daylight. "All that for…" He trailed off as he saw Kaylin stripping off her leather armor. "Uh…Kaylin?"

"What?" she asked, pulling her bandage free, the stained white cloth fluttering in the breeze. Across from them, a startled merchant swore as he smacked into a lantern pole, his attention fully encompassed by the half-dressed elf, who was now shrugging her armor back on. "My wound is healed, so I don't need it anymore." Her huge green eyes looked over at him. "Could you strap me up, partner?"

"Ah…right," he said, stepping closer and cinching her armor tight. *Her hair smells like pine trees,* he thought to himself. "Speaking of which, we're out of bandages now, and I don't have a whole lot else. A few mixed healing herbs just in case, a rusty dagger I found along the road, and a bit of iron ore I've been meaning to sell. What I'm saying is…we need to get some supplies. What do you have with you?"

"Besides my bow and knife?" Kaylin asked, turning around to face him and adjusting her armor. "Well, fourteen arrows and seven arrenroot flowers."

"Arrenroot?" Vexx frowned. "I'm not very familiar with herbs. What properties does it have?"

"Properties?" Kaylin grinned. "I mean, they're pretty! I've just been picking them as I go along. So where's the market?"

Vexx sighed internally and led her down the street.

"Well, maybe they'll come in handy. You think you could learn how to make healing poultices?"

"Nah," Kaylin said casually as she strode by, kicking a stone out of the way, bits of mud spattering in the air. "I just want to get better at archery. Traps too. I did some thinking after that last fight, and ever since I woke up, I've had this idea for a trap that I really want to try out. We could use it on our goblin friend!"

"Well…what if we get wounded? How will we heal up?"

"You're the mage," she said with a laugh. "Anyway, if you don't want to heal, we'll just pick up some potions."

"I'm out of money…" Vexx grumbled. "The barkeep has everything I had. What do you have?"

"Money…money…" Kaylin said to herself, sounding out the word. "That's a human thing, right?"

Vexx buried his face in his hands as they entered the market district. Shouting voices echoed over the clanging of Cloudbury's forge. The traffic was thicker here, a wagon passing by laden with lumber, a couple of mounted caravan guards beside it. *That's a good job,* Vexx thought as he slowly lowered his hands. *It isn't raiding dungeons, but it's steady pay and a bit of excitement if they come across any goblins or bandits.*

"Yes, money!" Vexx finally replied as they passed a food stand. "You need it for, well, for everything!"

"Oh…that explains why those villagers were chasing me the other day…" Kaylin mused. "I guess they thought the carrots growing in their field were just for them."

Vexx raised his head. "Did they put a bounty on you?" He smirked. "Maybe I could collect."

"Sure, if you want," she said with a cheery smile. "What's a bounty, anyway?"

Before Vexx could respond, they rounded the corner into the town's bazaar. In prime position was a tall man with a forked beard, pointing proudly at a large snuffling lizard with an attached saddle. Beside him stood a black woman in a flowing green dress who nodded in satisfaction as she sized up the beast.

"Highly resistant to disease, ma'am, and none too picky about what it eats."

"Good, good," she replied. Vexx wondered if she was a more experienced dungeoneer. She didn't seem to be around here, or to be an academy graduate for that matter. His vision was blocked by an armored knight striding past, warhammer resting on a shoulder, and then he winced as Kaylin squealed beside him.

"Ooh, pets!"

Kaylin weaved through the crowd and smiled as she put her hand in front of a horse, who warily sniffed at it. Vexx grabbed her other hand and pulled her away.

"They're *mounts*, and there's no way we could afford even one of them. Not like either of us know the first thing about riding one."

"I could learn," Kaylin huffed indignantly.

"For now, let's stick to potions, alright?"

9

DOCTOR FANSEE'S PICK-ME-UPS

The potion stall was unoccupied, an oasis of calm in the busy Cloudbury market. Vexx frowned as he stood there. Vials sat on the wooden booth, one a swirling mix of black and purple, the others of simpler reds, greens, and blues. The sign read Doctor Fansee's Pick-Me-Ups, but the doctor did not appear to be in.

"Hello?" Vexx asked.

A mop of springy white hair emerged from behind the counter, and then the creased and wrinkled face of a gnome appeared, blinking at them from behind thick-rimmed glasses. "Oh, a customer! I didn't see you up there. I was just—" A pop sounded from below, swirling green smoke clouded the air, and the gnome coughed for a few seconds as he waved the acrid smoke away. "That's a bad batch of Fenriconian mushrooms, make no mistake. Anyway, what can I do for you?"

"We'll need a health potion. We're hunting a goblin!" Kaylin announced proudly.

The gnome stared at her for a second and let out an incredulous laugh. "*A* goblin? Just one?"

"Oh yes, but I've heard he's strong. He's killed several sheep! So Vexx thinks we'll need some potions."

"I'm...well..." Vexx stammered, flustered from the poorly disguised chortles from the nearby crowd. "It's just...safety first."

"Yes, yes," the gnome said, unsuccessfully hiding his amusement. "Goblins are certainly fearsome, especially when they're on their own. Do you think you'll need two?"

"Oh, I don't know!" Kaylin looked over at Vexx. "What do you think, Vexx? Do you think we'll need two health potions for one goblin? Why's everyone laughing?"

"Just the one, thanks," Vexx said between gritted teeth. *They might laugh now, but soon they'll know my name when I'm on par with Dred Wyrm.*

"Hmm..." the gnome slid a small red potion across the stall but kept his gaze locked on Vexx. "You're a mage, aren't you?"

"I am, indeed."

The gnome tapped a small blue vial, the sound ringing out. "Why don't you get one of these bad boys? I bet they never let you use mana potions in the Academy. I see you're wearing Initiate's robes. Let me guess, you dropped out?"

Vexx grimaced. "The instructors just couldn't handle my brilliance...oh, never mind. And yes, I've tried mana potion before. It's like drinking ectoplasm mixed with dwarven moonshine."

"Well, I add spearmint in mine. How's your stamina?" the gnome looked over at Kaylin and gave her a lecherous wink. "I'll bet he could use more with you around, am I right?"

"Hmm?" She blinked. "Yes, I suppose Vexx could use more stamina."

Vexx muttered something unintelligible and wished for the ground to open up and swallow him.

"Oh, don't worry," she said with a smile. "I was also exhausted last night! By the time you put me to bed—"

"That's not…she's just…"

"Don't worry, partner, I'll get this one," Kaylin said as she carefully set out a few copper pieces. "I forgot I had these little bits of metal."

The gnome smiled. "Aren't you a darling? Any time you get more bits of metal, come back and see Doctor Fansee's Pick-Me-Ups. Any potions you want; competitively priced, guaranteed 99% poison free!"

"Sure. Who's that?"

The gnome frowned in confusion and pointed up at his sign. Kaylin tilted her head as she squinted at it.

"Doc…tor…"

"You're a lucky man," the gnome said in a quiet voice as he slid over the vial. "Just keep in mind, the Church doesn't like interracial interc—"

"I'm not," Vexx sputtered, glancing at Kaylin, who was still sounding out the sign. "I'm not sleeping with her," he said in a quieter voice.

The gnome nodded, clearly unconvinced. "Do I look like a paladin to you, buddy? I don't care what you do. Just let me know if it lasts for more than four hours. Sometimes I mess up the dosage."

10

POLLANDER'S SHEEP

"A right up here," Kaylin said for the tenth time as they strode along the main road outside Cloudbury. "I know, I know," Vexx snapped.

"Okay, because last time—"

"I know!"

They turned and continued in silence, passing the three scattered homesteads that Pollander described. Based on the tranquil scene, it was hard to imagine that any goblin raiding had happened around here. At least, not lately. *Though I've always heard it's a rough country near the Lifeless Hills. As if farming and ranching wasn't hard enough.*

Kaylin's left ear twitched. "There are some sheep up ahead. They sound scared."

By the time they reached the third house, Vexx could make out the bleating with his own ears. They were penned in a small enclosure, a pitchfork sticking out of a pile of hay nearby, but the area was otherwise quiet. The two dungeoneers separated and approached the area in silence, though it didn't take long before the two of them met again in the close-cropped field.

Flies buzzed around the half-devoured carcass of a sheep. Blood and drag marks indicated that at least a second sheep had been killed, though the trail of blood disappeared into the underbrush leading up to the Lifeless Hills. Vexx let out a whistle as he squatted down beside the sheep.

"Looks like our little fella had himself a meal here and took another one away for later."

"Really?" Kaylin asked. "You asked the sheep that?"

"What?"

"You said you trained in the Dark Arts, right? Are you asking the sheep's ghost questions?"

Vexx blinked in surprise...then looked down at the sheep. A thought rose in his mind. *That elf might be the dumbest person I've ever come across. And yet...*his hand hovered over the sheep's skull. *And yet...*

Vexx bit his lip and stood up. "No. I'm just guessing based on the blood trail. Do you see the way the grass is bent over in one direction? He carried the second sheep away."

"Oh, right," Kaylin said, nodding agreeably. "I guess that could be it."

"No time like the present," Vexx said, already trotting away and following the trail of upturned grass and drops of blood. He felt excitement rising in him as he continued the hunt. *To kill or be killed...and we have an advantage over our foe. A goblin might be starting out small, but if we hurry, we'll be back well before nightfall, and then I can leave this damned village for good.*

He glanced over at Kaylin as they walked, the lithe elf stepping lightly through the bushes and scattered trees. Her tanned skin and dull leather armor blended in well here, the earthy browns would hide her easily as the colors of the grass shifted from greens to yellows. Vexx tried to recall what he knew of the elves.

They live in tree villages, like she'd said. I wonder, though, are they all as naive as her? She's handy with a bow, at least, and moves with an athletic gra—

"Oof!"

Kaylin tripped, sliding down a sloping hill, her bow jutting out as it caught on branches and rocks. Vexx snickered despite himself, then kept his face blank as he carefully stepped down the slope, bits of dirt falling around him. Kaylin cursed and muttered as she slowly got to her feet.

"Careful here," Vexx said. "It's a rocky country outside of Cloudbury."

Kaylin nodded. "The Lifeless Hills, right? You're from around here, aren't you, Vexx? Why are they called that?"

Vexx let out a long sigh. "Well, it's true there are goblins and wild animals around, but it's no place for humans to make a living. Not for long. We just stick around the edge of the forest."

"The logging camps," Kaylin said, nodding to herself. "They're not so far from my tree village."

"Why'd you leave, anyway?" Vexx asked as Kaylin dusted off her knees. They began walking down the trail again. The trail was harder to follow now, with only the occasional drag marks and spots of blood to guide them. The air seemed thinner as well, Vexx took in long breaths as he continually scanned the trees and brush around them.

"To seek fame and fortune," Kaylin said. "What about you?"

"Ah, well..." Vexx trailed off, unpleasant memories of his time at the Academy coming back to him. It hadn't been all bad, of course, and he'd learned magic. Not a lot of people had the kind of talent he had, or the drive to learn more...even if that very ambition was what brought his time at the Academy to an end.

"Something like that," he said after a moment. "Be the next Dred Wyrm, you know? The best dungeoneer around," he said, almost defensively, and glanced over at Kaylin as if afraid she'd laugh. Instead, she just looked over thoughtfully.

"That's a good ambition. I wish you the best of luck."

Vexx grinned. *She might be a bit stupid and naive, but at least she's nice. There could be worse people to go into battle with.*

Kaylin scrambled up a ridge, raising her hand to her eyes, and Vexx found his gaze locking onto her. *Not a bad-looking sort either.*

"Vexx!" The elf glanced over, her bright eyes iridescent in the light, and she grinned widely when she got his attention. "I found the sheep!"

11

SETTING THE TRAP

Kaylin worked intently with her cords, muttering under her breath as she tied one end of a rope to a branch. Vexx peered over, looking past the dead sheep and towards the nearest cave. They'd poked around the entrance and found several other caves nearby before Kaylin had eagerly suggested setting up a trap. Vexx found he preferred the idea of setting up an ambush here over going down below and so he stood there, scouting around, as Kaylin finished setting up her snare trap.

"And then...there! Once he steps beside the sheep, we'll get him for sure."

"You're sure about this?" Vexx asked, trying to keep the skepticism out of his voice.

"Of course," she said, completely focused on tying a knot. Vexx shrugged and wandered over to a hollow with an overhang where he'd made the most basic of shelters. A fire would be easy for him to start, of course, but they had to keep a low profile here. Vexx gathered up some dried grass, wedged himself into concealment, and resolved to have himself a pleasant nap.

CRACK!

Vexx's eyes snapped open. Kaylin was beside him, softly snoring into his ear, and he quickly shook her awake. "I hear something," he hissed as the elf shook off her sleepiness. It was just past dawn, the first faint glimmers of light appearing above the nearby ridge.

Did I really sleep that long? Vexx wondered as he scrubbed wetness off his cheek. *Elf slobber. Gross.*

The same grunting and shuffling that he'd heard earlier were growing louder now. He squinted to make out shapes in the darkness, but as usual, Kaylin spotted it first.

"The goblin," she whispered beside him, hurriedly rummaging for her bow, and quietly stringing it. "He's by the trap! He's got the sheep...and...he's dragging it," she said, readying a shot. Vexx had kept his clothes on over the night, needing little else, but waited to summon a flame.

Ice bolts are alright if I'm putting out a fire, and I've been taught quite a few other tricks. But fireballs? There's no beating it.

"What? He's gone right past the...agh, why didn't it work!"

The shuffling stopped at this. Then it grew louder, more panicked, and now Vexx could dimly make out the goblin dragging the sheep to one of the cave entrances.

"Great going, Kaylin," Vexx said, visibly annoyed that the element of surprise had gone. "You spooked him!"

Fire flamed into life below his hands, illuminating the elf as she huffed beside him. "Well, I'm going to get him! Follow me!"

Kaylin bounded off, heedless of the rocks in the darkness around her, while Vexx followed along at a slower pace, scanning the ground as he walked forward. Soon, a shriek tore through his thoughts and he glanced up as Kaylin soared into the air.

12

INTO THE CAVE

The flames pouring from his palms illuminated the twisted, struggling elf trapped in her net, bouncing up and down between the limbs of two sturdy pine trees. It came to a rest and she was well and truly stuck, her arms and legs jutted out of the nets as she desperately tried to struggle free.

"Nice job, elf!" Vexx whistled.

"Don't just stand there!" she called down.

"Never fear, Kaylin, I have a goblin to catch."

"At least cut me down!"

"No time for that," Vexx snapped as he hurried ahead.

"Vexx!"

The goblin had disappeared into one of the cave entrances, the deceptively strong creature holding the sheep over one shoulder, but Vexx followed close behind, sprinting through the winding tunnel.

I have to catch up soon, before the corridor splits in two or three. Then there'd be no way we'd catch him in time!

Vexx was close enough that he saw rocks still rolling from where the goblin and his captured sheep had dislodged them, and even a few bloodstains along stalactites where the dead sheep had brushed across them. He strained forward, leaping ahead as the path twisted and went deeper into the mountain, a faint emerald glow emerging around them. The chamber opened up now, and even in his hurry, Vexx faltered at the sight.

He slowed, choosing his steps carefully. The dim glow fell on the carcass of the sheep, abandoned in the middle of the passage. The glow seemed to give the white wool a peculiar greenish tinge, but Vexx thought he saw something crouching behind it.

"Come out, you filthy creature!" Vexx shouted as he peered over the sheep's carcass. Goblins were short and cunning creatures, but it was little use hiding behind the dead sheep. He leaned over, a flame readied. The goblin wasn't there.

"What the—"

Vexx glanced up just as a snarling goblin leaped at him from atop a massive stalactite. He reeled to the side, the goblin's axe missing, but the creature had already sunk its teeth into Vexx's shoulder. Vexx screamed in pain, instinctively grabbing the goblin with both his hands and tearing it off before throwing it to the side.

He raised both hands now, just as the goblin spun around. It approached menacingly with an axe in its hand and a twisted scowl on its misshapen face. Flames burst forward, a powerful spray of fire that burned the goblin to a crisp. Vexx couldn't suppress his yell of pain and agony as the fire tore into the goblin.

Then he ended the spell.

In a flash, the fire dimmed, and smoke rose from a few smoldering fires around the blackened corpse of the goblin. Vexx sagged down to one knee and stared at the fire-blackened body for a long moment.

"Shit."

Now that he had a second to think, Vexx realized that the ruined figure in front of him would be hard to explain as a goblin. He scanned from left to right, exhaustion slowing his motions, and rocked back on his heels in dismay.

"Shit," Vexx repeated.

I need a drink.

He patted at his robe, smiling as he felt the potion still in his pocket. *It was good thinking to keep this here instead of in my pack.* Vexx raised it up, the blue liquid looking almost teal in the glow of the emerald crystals that dotted the ceiling, and popped open the cork. Vexx took a few greedy swigs before corking it and placing it back in his robes.

Better save some of that for later.

"Ah, that's the stuff," Vexx said to himself, his voice echoing in the massive chamber, then burped as he felt his stomach rumble. He certainly felt more energetic, at least. A band of a dozen goblins could have rounded the corner just then and Vexx knew he'd be able to send fireballs flying at every one of them if he needed to.

Instead, the cavern was as quiet as ever.

Vexx leaned in close, noticing now that one side of the goblin's face had been less burned than the other, as the creature had twisted away in pain. He held his disgust in as he turned it to the side and grinned as he saw one of the goblin's ears was just slightly charred. Vexx produced his knife and pressed it against the ear.

He hesitated a moment.

Dred Wyrm wouldn't hesitate. Dred Wyrm must have done this a thousand times.

Vexx gritted his teeth and cut away, pulling the severed ear off a moment later.

"There," he said, his voice echoing in the cave. "All the proof we need."

I hope.

Vexx stood up now, pocketing his trophy, and scanned the open cavern. The corridor had come to an end here, the massive rock walls pocked and spotted with lichen and the glowing emerald crystals. Yet in one corner, Vexx saw another glow—a faint, pulsing violet light that he expected to be Breithian cave mushrooms.

So that's why the goblin turned and fought. There was no escape for him in here. The barkeep mentioned looking for loot—I wonder if he has anything in here?

Vexx paused in thought for a moment, wondering if Kaylin was still struggling to free herself outside. Then he shrugged. *A couple more minutes won't hurt her.*

Vexx walked over, following the violet glow of the massive mushrooms.

13

THE DEAD ADVENTURER

The picked-over carcass of a sheep lay beside an empty bed of straw. Vexx sniffed. Mixed with the cool, mildewy smell of the entire cavern was a foul stench Vexx was beginning to recognize as goblin.

"Must have been a hungry fella," Vexx said to himself, prodding the sheep carcass and bed with his boot, but there seemed little of value there. He shifted his gaze over to a collection of bones and other assorted trash. Some of the bones looked distinctly human, bits of faded leather rotting away on the body, and Vexx squatted beside it.

"Let's see…"

He turned the skeleton over, the bones light in his hands, and grinned as he felt a pack. He wrenched it loose from the skeleton. Vexx wasn't bothered much by being around corpses, not since his experiments with the Black Arts, and it was clear this adventurer had been dead for a very long time.

The faint glow of the emerald crystals and the nearby grove of luminescent violet mushrooms didn't provide much in the way of light, however, and Vexx was growing increasingly guilty about leaving Kaylin on her own. So he grabbed the pack for himself, along with what looked to be a rotting quiver. He scanned the ground again, glancing at the Breithian cave mushrooms.

I have no idea what they're for, but they might be worth a few coppers to the right person.

Vexx quickly cut away a few stalks, casting a dubious gaze at a nearby glowing crystalline rock, but gave up after a few tugs.

A dwarf with a pickaxe might pry it loose, but I've spent enough time here.

Vexx turned back down the corridor, humming to himself as he went along, following the twists and turns that led him back outside. He winced as he came to the cave opening, the light bright and uncomfortable as he emerged. It was fully daylight now.

A series of curses brought his attention back up to Kaylin, who was still struggling in her net. "That you, Vexx?" she called out, hanging in the net strung between two sturdy tree limbs. "Where have you been?"

"Solved our goblin problem while you've been playing around," Vexx replied, walking under her.

Her legs were twisted to the side, bow jutting out behind her, and every time she wriggled helplessly, her whole body rocked back and forth in her net. She managed to lean down the side and glared as Vexx whistled.

"Are you looking up my outfit?"

"Wouldn't dream of it," Vexx lied. *It's really quite the view. Still, I should probably do something about that.*

"So, I've been thinking," Kaylin said, attempting to gesture at one of the two tree limbs that held here. "If you were to climb up and carefully cut away at the—"

Two fireballs flew up, bursting into the tree limbs and severing them with a crack. Kaylin shrieked as she fell to the ground in front of Vexx. The elf struggled in the net, indignantly swiping away the rope and debris as she got to her feet.

"Vexx, I swear…"

"What?" Vexx shrugged. "I got you down. More than that, I got you a few presents," he added, setting the aged pack down on the ground and handing the quiver over as if it were a peace offering. "I found a dead adventurer in that cave. The wood has faded away, but there's a few decent steel arrowheads here. You can have those. Next time we're in town, we'll stop by the fletcher."

Kaylin took them and pouted with a sullen look on her face. "I still can't believe you just left me there while you rummaged around in the cave."

Vexx shrugged. "That's what you get for getting caught in your own trap."

"At least I know it works," she muttered. "Next time, I'll get 'em for sure!"

Vexx had set the pack down and now took a closer look, raising a black stone in the air and squinting at it in the morning light. "What's this?"

"Flint. For starting fires."

Vexx snorted and tossed it into a nearby bush. "Don't need it."

"Vexx!"

He rummaged through a multitude of faded odds and ends and then pulled out an ancient leather scroll. Vexx whistled at the discovery. He unrolled the adventurer's aged scroll and frowned as he tried to make out the words. Kaylin hummed beside him.

"I can't read human writing. What does it say, Vexx?"

"This appears to be a log. Fairly boring, really, though it seems he used to be a dungeoneer. It's mostly lists of provisions and complaints about mushroom stew. Hang on, what's this?" Vexx furrowed his brow at the weather-worn passage. "Something about a 'Ruby of the Pure.' And…blah blah blah, something about a trap, and then…'great power'?"

They glanced at each other, their eyebrows raised.

14

THE FIRST JOB

Vexx wrinkled his nose for the hundredth time. "It stinks."

"It's just a little ear," Kaylin retorted, flashing a smile at Vexx as they continued their walk back into Cloudbury. "At least it's not a nose. That would be really smelly."

Vexx glanced over, unsure if Kaylin was joking, but her deep green eyes looked earnest and serious.

"What?" she asked after a moment.

"Never mind," he muttered. "Anyway, this Ruby of the Pure. Have you ever heard anything about it?"

"Nope!"

"Hmm…" Vexx mused, then shrugged to himself. "Well, never mind that. We're almost back to Cloudbury and closer to payment for our first successful dungeoneering job! Never mind the burning barn, those goblins we killed, and you getting wounded and then trapped, and that bear we just ran away from…"

"It was huge!" Kaylin squeaked indignantly.

"It sure was," Vexx said with a firm nod. "But anyway, that's past us now, and soon we'll be on to the next one.

You know, they say nine out of ten dungeoneers die within their first ten missions. But we just got one step closer!"

"Oh…" Kaylin said, looking sad.

Vexx glanced over. "Did you not know that?"

"Did you know them?" she asked. "I'm sorry you lost nine friends, Vexx."

Vexx fell silent, trying to think of something to say. Instead, he just shook his head. By the time he raised it, they were at the outskirts of Cloudbury, the raucous sounds of the market rising up, mixing with the shouts and rhythmic thudding of axes, courtesy of the nearby loggers. His spirits lifted as his boots slapped on the soft cobblestones of Cloudbury itself, a smile filling his face as—

"Hey, Vexxy!"

Vexx stiffened as he glanced over at a huge red bearded logger, an enormous grin plastered on the man's face. A moment later, Vexx blinked in shock as he recognized the man. They'd just been boys then, but they had grown up together. Before Vexx had been accepted into the magical academy.

"Tad Armstrong," Vexx muttered. "I guess it's good to see you."

"Hah! You don't have to pretend with me," he said, grinning over at Kaylin. "Hey, Miss! Has Vexxy told you about all the wedgies I gave him?"

Kaylin blinked. "Is that a fruit?"

"I'm busy, Tad," Vexx snapped. "I'm a dungeoneer now, if you didn't know."

"Oh, are ya?" Tad scratched his beard in thought. "I heard you got expelled from the Magical Academy for doing stuff with corpses."

Vexx grimaced, glancing at the onlookers around him.

"First of all, what I was doing was research, which those *cowards* were unwilling to…you know what? I don't have time for this." He tugged at Kaylin's arm. "Let's go."

"See you around, buddy!" Tad called out as Vexx stormed away towards the tavern, mumbling to himself as he dragged Kaylin along with him.

"I was building on Mistress Sarcafaulantris's undead investigations," Vexx grumbled to no one in particular. "Literally making groundbreaking advancements in necrology, and yet—"

"Hey, Vexx?"

Vexx glanced back and let go of Kaylin's arm. "What?"

"You just walked past the door," Kaylin said, jerking her thumb back at the tavern entrance, rowdy noises echoing out of it. "And what's a wedgie? Can I try one some time?"

"Yeah, sure thing," Vexx muttered, pushing open the tavern door and walking past a party of dwarves engaged in a drinking contest. The air smelled thick here, but it was an improvement on the rank stench of the goblin ear, and Vexx lost no time in approaching the bar counter. A silver-haired elf in rich merchant's robes finished his order, clasping an iron cup filled with red wine, and then Vexx was face to face with the barkeep.

The older man raised an eyebrow. "So did you get him?"

"What does this look like?" Vexx asked triumphantly, all but tossing the goblin ear on the counter.

Pollander sniffed. "Well, it looks like a pig ear, but it smells like shit." He tilted his head and poked it. "It's burnt too. What are you playing at, kid?"

"It's a goblin ear."

The barkeep snorted. "Like all the hells it is. Goodman

Harolds sells pig ears just like this down on Main Street. If you think I'm going to—"

"I hate to butt in," a high-pitched voice said, and together, Vexx and the barkeep glanced over at the elf merchant, who was carefully sipping his wine. "But I have a very keen sense of smell. That is clearly a goblin ear, and unless my senses desert me entirely…" he paused and sniffed again. "That's the left ear. Mountain goblin, from the Lifeless Hills. I'm detecting a whiff of Breithian cave mushroom as well."

Vexx grinned, nodding at the man. "Thank you!" He looked back at the barkeep. "See?"

The barkeeper nodded reluctantly.

"And also, a hint of juniper," the elf continued. "And perhaps oak?"

"Ah, that would be the drink, sir," Pollander cut in. "Aged in oak barrels they are, with a touch of juniper."

"Oh." The elf blinked, glancing down at his drink. "So it is."

Pollander drummed his thick fingers on the counter. "Alright, well I'm glad that rascal was dealt with. Let me get you your coins."

Vexx nodded to himself, then looked over to see Kaylin appear next to him. "Where'd you go?" he asked.

Kaylin frowned. "Well…if you must know, I went to powder my ears. A bit of freshening up wouldn't hurt you either."

Before Vexx could reply, the barkeep had returned and coins clanked onto the counter. "Fifteen, like we agreed on."

Vexx scooped them up and handed one over to Kaylin, who blinked down at them in surprise. "That's half?"

"Yes, after you consider the initial investment of

course." Vexx said, looking back at the barkeep. "Got another job for us?"

"As it happens, I do have a job for someone of your astoundingly meager talents," he said, then glanced at Kaylin. "But you're not going to like it."

15

DISCOUNT FASHION

Vexx browsed through Market Street, still thinking about the barkeep's words. Pollander hadn't been shy about calling the old man who'd put the request in a 'strange, old creep.' Still, it was a job…of sorts. And that meant experience along with a few coins. Vexx stuck his hand in his pocket and felt the solid weight of the coins.

My first dungeoneering haul, and here I am about to spend it all.

Kaylin and Vexx had split up to do their own shopping, though Vexx was not entirely sure she'd be safe on her own.

Time to sharpen up my wardrobe, anyway. I left the Magical Academy for good. It's time I got myself a dungeoneering outfit.

Vexx shuffled through the racks at a cheap vendor, pausing at a white tunic. Or pinkish, anyway, with noticeable splotches. He poked his finger through a tear near the top.

"Gently used," the vendor commented.

"I see. You took this off a corpse?"

The vendor shot him a look. "Never mind where I took it from."

Vexx shrugged after a moment. "It's fine. Doesn't bother me. I think I'll stick with black, though," he said, patting his worn black robes.

The vendor nodded, waving him over. "Come around the back, let's see what I have."

Vexx stepped through the musty interior, the aged wood creaking under his feet, casting his eyes in wonder at the headgear around. A sultan's hat with a peacock feather, a solid steel helmet with a dent on one side, a shimmering magical hat of some strange design. Subconsciously, Vexx ran his fingers through his chestnut brown hair, eyeing a collection of bandanas.

That's about all I could afford. For now, let's stick to the robes.

He bent down and stepped into an adjoining room where the vendor was perusing dark-colored robes. He bent down and sniffed a dark purple robe.

"Frost resistant," the vendor said as he hovered nearby. "This one is also known to boost your proficiency at healing."

Vexx snorted. "It's almost summer, and I'm no healer. Besides, purple isn't black. Get me something that says—" he snapped his fingers and cocked a brow at the shop owner as flames burst from the tip of his pointer finger, "badass dungeoneer on the prowl."

The vendor shot a worried look over his shoulder. "Kindly keep your fire away from the merchandise." As the fire disappeared, the vendor nodded to himself. "I think I have something for you. Let's see…"

A few minutes later, Vexx White stepped out, smiling broadly as he felt the smooth silk of one long sleeve. The black fabric shimmered with a dark green hue that the vendor assured him was poison that would latch on to anyone foolish enough to attack him up close.

"But it only works…" the vendor shifted his hand back and forth vaguely. "Ehh, sometimes. But you see how the red trim complements your fire magic? And your eyes as well, sir, if you pardon me saying so. How does the gentleman like it?"

Vexx whistled appreciatively, popping his collar like he'd seen the cool kids at the Magical Academy do. *How do you like me now?* He glanced at his reflection and wordlessly set his coins on the counter.

"I feel like half pimp, half warlock in this."

"Very good, sir," the vendor said, collecting his coins. "Mind how you go."

Lost in thought, Vexx took a few steps outside the building and into the crowd before he recognized the voice hailing him.

"Hey Vexx, nice robes!"

Vexx turned around and blinked. "Whoa. Ah…whoa."

Kaylin tilted her head and looked a little bashful. The light reflected off the studded leather that covered her breasts and little else. Beneath her exposed midriff was a dark brown leather skirt, and her feet were encased in gladiator sandals of the same material going midway up her tanned calves.

"It's not elven style," she said after a moment, "but it's an upgrade at least. What do you think?"

Vexx swallowed. "I think it looks good."

"Yeah…I preferred full coverage, but the seller said that less armor means better protection." She shrugged. "He even gave me a discount to try it on. Why should I pass that up?"

Leather crinkled and strained as she raised her shoulders in a shrug.

"Good point," Vexx said. "Are you done picking up supplies? I'm ready now."

"Sure! It was just this and a few arrows, anyway. That goblin money didn't last very long."

Vexx nodded, already leading the way to the building the barkeep had indicated. "Let's hope rats are more profitable."

16

OLD MAN

The door creaked open and Vexx stood in the doorway, his hand in the air, mid-knock. Standing in the gloom was a wizened old man who blinked rheumy eyes at them. He clutched a wooden staff, either for protection or support, Vexx couldn't tell. The old man tilted his head at Vexx.

"Are you Death?"

Vexx grinned, smoothing out his shimmering black robe. "No, but I like the compliment. We're here because the barkeep said you had a rat problem."

"We?" the old man asked, and Vexx shifted aside. The old man's eyes boggled as he took in Kaylin, who waved shyly at him.

"Hi there, sir! What can I do for you?"

"Easy, Kaylin," Vexx said in a low voice, taking in the old man's lecherous gaze. "We don't want to give him a heart attack."

"Ooh, I like you," the old man said after a moment, sucking on his few remaining teeth. "You'll do just nicely! Come on in," he said, stepping back. "I meant her," he muttered as Vexx stepped in first, ducking through the door and entering the main room.

It was a drab interior, cobwebs coating the edges, and the walls had a faintly yellowish sheen to them. Motes of dust drifted down from a nearby bookshelf, a couple wooden chairs, a table, and a rickety ladder were the only other objects of note in the interior. Vexx cleared the way as the old man gestured for Kaylin to enter.

"Pardon the mess. My wife passed away, you see, and certain things have gone…untended to," the old man said.

"Just show me what needs doing," Kaylin replied with a smile.

"Ooh…"

"And Vexx and I will get right on it!"

"Oh…" The old man sounded decidedly less excited and blinked over at Vexx. "You know what, young man? I have something else for you to do. Some rats have gotten into my cellar and I'd like them cleared out. It's very cramped, so it's best if you handle it alone."

Vexx raised his eyebrows.

"Oh, don't be like that, sonny," the old man replied after a long moment. "There's a great treasure in my cellar. You're welcome to it once you clear them out. Your friend here can help me with something else."

"Fine. I'll get your rats."

The things I do for a few coppers. Still, a job's a job.

He gave a brief nod, then went down the staircase. There was a solid wooden door leading to the cellar with a wrought iron handle on it. Vexx paused, crouching down and listening beside it. He heard Kaylin titter at something the old man must have said, but he put them out of his mind.

She's a grown woman, she can handle herself.

Vexx thought he could faintly hear skittering down below along with what sounded like broken glass. He clasped a hand around the handle and hauled it up. In a flash, a ball of circling flame emerged around his fist, casting a dim light on the cellar below. Something rustled as it darted back, pausing a moment to look up at Vexx, dim red eyes shining in reflection. Then it scurried away.

"Come back, little rat," Vexx called out, already stepping down the staircase into the cellar, waving away cobwebs that threatened to get entangled in his hair. "I just want to say hi."

The light reflected off a dusty mirror, and Vexx could make out a few ancient pieces of furniture, along with a shelf that held quite a lot of glassware. Below it was a puddle that sparked even as he squinted; a multicolored hue that almost seemed to move as he looked. That could only mean one thing.

Potions. Damn, the rats must have gotten into them.

Vexx stepped forward cautiously, expelling more energy into the circling ball of fire, further illuminating the dusty cellar. He saw another reflection of red eyes and grinned even as he readied his fireball. Then, he realized the eyes were much higher than before. And others emerged…four, six, a dozen…

Vexx let loose with a fireball, hitting what appeared to be a giant rat full in the face, and in a flash, he saw the other snarling creatures massed together.

What in all the hells is this!? Those aren't normal rats!

Before he could stop and think, the giant rats charged forward in a snarling stampede, and Vexx let loose with frantic fireballs from both hands. The wounded rats shrieked as they reeled to the sides, their flesh burned and blackened. The other ones simply ran over their smoldering corpses, their beady eyes trained on Vexx. Vexx braced both hands together, releasing his fan of flames, a wave of burning fire that swept outward in a V shape. The giant rats squealed even as they staggered forward, one of them somehow evading the flames as it leaped over another dying rat.

Vexx stumbled back, exhausted as his flames fell away. A few seconds was all it took for the last rat to hit him full in the chest and sink its teeth into his shoulder. His robes emitted a dull green glow and he cried out just as the rat recoiled and staggered back in shock. The giant rat shook its head as if in disbelief, coughing and sputtering, and Vexx poured the last of his energy into a swirling fireball.

So the poison effect really does work.

He hurled the fireball forward, watching as the explosion flung the last giant rat back into the wooden shelf, knocking potions and vials in all directions. The rat slumped to the ground in the pile of broken glass and flickering magical liquid. Vexx breathed out slowly and felt for his shoulder. A few fires still burned on the fur of the fallen giant rats.

Vexx stepped forward, kicking the last giant rat square in the stomach. It made no move. "You rat bastard. I can't believe you bit me." Vexx pulled his robe back, squinting at the bite mark and grimaced as he saw a faint trickle of blood.

He scanned the shelf for the few remaining potions, noticing a half-full jug of moonshine. Vexx popped the cork and gave it a few tentative sniffs before pouring it liberally on his wounded shoulder. He gritted his teeth at the burning sensation and took a long drink for good measure.

Vexx set it back with a long sigh. A couple other red

and blue-hued vials remained and Vexx quickly pocketed them.

The old man hadn't mentioned they were giant rats, after all. I'm entitled to a bit of a bonus. And speaking of bonuses...

Vexx scanned the cellar for whatever the old man might consider to be great treasure. There was little of value besides the dusty mirror, a slumped-over bookshelf that was partly charred from a stray fireball, and a half-collapsed desk. He approached the desk and slid open the drawers. At the bottom, he caught the gleam of a lockbox and smiled as he hefted it atop the desk. Vexx sparked a new light as the smoldering giant rat carcasses faded into blackness.

He rattled the lockbox, noting that it was still locked. There was a place for a key and Vexx knew a skilled lock-picker might make the attempt. *It might be worth learning how to do that in the future,* Vexx thought, grabbing the lockbox and making his way back up the stairs. *But for now, I'll just have the old man open it.*

Vexx staggered up the stairs and rounded the corner into the main room. He stopped and took in the scene. Kaylin was perched on a ladder, humming happily to herself as she dusted a bookcase, and behind her, the old man grinned as he stared up at her skirt.

"Hey, dirty old man!" Vexx snapped, and the old man looked over guiltily. "I took care of your rats, you creep. Or should I say, your *giant* rats. You didn't mention they got into your potions."

"Eh? Well that's why I offered the job. If they were little rats, I'd just squish 'em with my staff."

"I'll take my reward now," Vexx snapped, glancing up

at Kaylin dusting away. "Kaylin, get down from there. We're dungeoneers, not maids."

"But I'm just about done!" she called out.

The old man was looking back up at her. "Yeah, sonny, she's just about done."

Vexx sighed, brushing cobwebs and dirt out of his hair, and slumped into a nearby wooden chair. He felt exhausted again after all that magic use. A moment later, Kaylin hopped down.

"I just fin—"

She was interrupted by the clattering sound of the books falling to the ground. Silence fell in the room for a moment.

"Oops."

17

GREAT TREASURE

The old man sighed. "Set those back up, missy, would you? I'll get that treasure," he said, walking over and muttering something about missing the view. The old man paused by Vexx and sniffed. "You smell like soot and liquor."

"You smell even worse," Vexx muttered, though the old man apparently didn't hear, instead shuffling away towards the cellar. Vexx sighed as Kaylin began stacking the books on the shelf. "I've seen corpses with more life than this guy," he said. "We've had better conversations, too."

"He seems nice enough," Kaylin replied. "He said I could come back whenever I wanted to do a job."

"I bet he wants you to polish his staff," Vexx remarked in a low voice.

"Well, I'm very good with my hands," Kaylin said nonchalantly as she set the last book in place. "There!" she said, stepping down from the ladder and dusting her hands. "Easy!"

"Easy? You didn't have to do anything," Vexx scoffed.

"I had to fight a bunch of giant rats!" Vexx tapped his finger on the lockbox beside him. He'd heard some rattles from within, and he knew there was definitely something inside. Still, the old man said his treasure was something else.

"What's that?" Kaylin asked as Vexx surreptitiously slid the lockbox into his pack.

"This? Oh, nothing. You don't happen to know how to pick locks, do you?"

Kaylin shrugged and shook her head.

I'll have to see if someone at the tavern is interested. I didn't fight all those giant rats just for a few lousy coins and a couple old potions. For a moment, Vexx briefly considered taking a swig of one of them. A healing elixir would help with his wound, though it really wasn't so bad, and the blue vial would help him recover his stamina after all that magic use.

No, best to just get over it. I'm feeling a bit better already, Vexx thought to himself, hauling himself out of the chair as the old man emerged from his basement. He fixed a cranky stare at Vexx.

"You ruined everything down there!"

Vexx snorted. "Did you see all those rats I killed?"

"Killed with fire magic," the old man snarled. "If I knew you'd burn half the cellar down I wouldn't have bothered. Back in my day, a young man would go down there with a hammer and a smile, and come back whistling a jaunty tune! You, well, look at you! You look like some sort of witch. This generation, I tell you…"

"You mentioned treasure?" Vexx prompted after a moment. *The sooner we get out of here the better.*

The old man's eyes snapped up and he held out a book, the cover partly burnt on one end. "Great treasure, I said, and more than the likes of you deserve. The rest of the payment is with the barkeep."

Vexx just stared out. "How about some gold? We'll take gold."

The old man snorted. "This is worth more than gold, if you have the wits to read it. Now get out of my house!"

"Oh, don't be like that!" Kaylin said as she approached. "We did our best!"

The old man's tone immediately softened, his eyes crinkling as he formed a half-smile. "Well. *You* were a delight. And any time you'd like an adventure, feel free to visit me! Heheh!"

Vexx hid his disgust as he took the offered book. "This isn't treasure," he muttered, briefly flipping through it, but the old man ignored him. *At least I kept his lockbox. There's bound to be a few things in there. Perhaps even some gold if we're lucky.*

"Come on, Kaylin," Vexx said as he grabbed Kaylin's arm, interrupting the old man in the middle of another lecherous remark. "Let's turn this one in."

18

EXPERT LOCKPICKER

Business in Cloudbury's tavern had died down. Vexx impatiently brushed bits of soot off his face as the barkeep returned with their meager payment. *It seems that killing rats isn't a profitable venture. Who knew?*

"So you got anything else—"

"Nope! That's all I've got for you," Pollander said with a shrug. "Look, Cloudbury is a small town and we've got small problems. Besides, if you want higher level tasks, you're going to have a lot more competition. You see those dwarves over there?" he asked, pointing at a party of drunken dwarves. "They just wiped out a handful of trolls down at Oerchenbrach. Now that will get you some real money, but let me tell you, there's quite a lot of risk involved. Not all the dwarves who started the adventure made it to the end, if you catch my meaning."

Vexx nodded.

"Where did they go?" Kaylin asked.

"Oh, sweetheart..." the barkeep said with a sigh, but moved down the counter to serve another customer.

"Well...what now, Vexx?"

Vexx drummed his fingers on the counter, lost in thought, but finally turned to Kaylin. "Do you want to stick with me, Kaylin? I mean, we could go our separate ways here if you want to. Doesn't seem like there's much demand for a couple of rookie dungeoneers."

"Do you want me to go?" Kaylin pouted, biting at her bottom lip, and Vexx shifted uncomfortably.

"Well, no…I'm just saying you could. If you wanted."

"No, we'll find something together, Vexx!"

"Good," Vexx replied, nodding his head and hefting his pack. "We still have a lockbox, a book, and a scroll to go over. I think it's time we did some proper dungeoneering. No odd jobs, but a quest of our own, to find some ancient loot and bring it back."

"Sounds great! Where should we start?"

"Ask around the tavern for someone who can pick locks," Vexx said, taking a seat on a bar stool and rummaging in his pack. "I'll go over the scroll and book. Barkeep!" He raised a finger as the older man glanced over. "I'll have a round. Reading is thirsty work."

&

A HALF-FULL MUG of ale stood neglected beside Vexx as he skimmed through the charred book, lost in thought. The scroll had proved useless, though it had certainly piqued his interest about the Ruby of the Pure. *That adventurer must have been nearby. It was clear his party had been looking for it. Did he get separated?*

As Vexx flipped a page, he felt the hair on the back of his neck stand on end—but it wasn't due to anything he read. All of his hair was rising in the air, which attracted a few bemused looks and comments from nearby patrons, and Vexx felt a strange frisson of magic thrum through him. *What the hell? Is this book ensorcelled?*

He flipped through page after page and noted several unfamiliar designs and symbols, but the ancient lettering was all but unrecognizable. Kaylin returned to find him still staring at the book.

"What's up with your hair?"

"Huh?"

Vexx blinked and set the book aside, the magical charge fading away as he put it down. "Oh. I was just…" he paused and shook his head. "I got a strange feeling from that book. Anyway, did you find our lockpicking expert?"

"Yeah, come on over!" Kaylin said, excitedly waving for him to join her, and Vexx hurriedly packed up his gear. Together, they made their way to the other side of the bar, where a dwarf with a trimmed black beard was grinning over at them. He hopped down from his chair as they approached.

"Put it over 'ere," he said, gesturing at the chair he'd just been sitting in. Vexx set the lockbox on the chair and glanced over.

"So, do you use little metal pins or—"

The dwarf's axe arced over and slammed into the lockbox, smashing the thin metal along with the chair below it, scattering splintered wood and metal all around them as nearby patrons cheered in amusement. Vexx grimaced, but it soon turned into a grin as he saw a few coins scattered in the debris, along with a few old necklaces and an amulet left inside the battered remains of the lockbox.

"I'll take a wee bit 'o your coin here, lad and lassie," the dwarf said, scooping up a heaping handful of coins and pausing to take a bite of a gleaming silver coin. He grinned up at them, even as Vexx and Kaylin began frantically gathering the rest up. "Now, I think it's time to be scamperin'."

"Hey, you there!" Vexx tossed the last of the coins in his pack as the barkeeper bellowed from across the tavern. "Don't you go breaking my chairs!"

"Let's go," Vexx snapped, and he grabbed Kaylin by the arm and led them out, scowling as the dwarf sprinted through the door to disappear in the crowd outside. "I thought you said he could pick locks! Dammit Kaylin, we might have to give this tavern a wide berth for a while."

"He said he could get it open for a share of the prize," Kaylin said with a shrug. "That's what you wanted, right?"

"I guess," Vexx conceded before he scanned the main street, then pulled her to the right. "It's just down here a ways. It should be around still," he said to himself, as they joined the boisterous midday traffic.

"What should?"

"A bookstore! I remember walking past it as a child. A magic book like this is bound to be worth something," he said, keeping a brisk pace even as he cast a worried look back at the tavern they'd just left.

"Let's go!"

19

THE HOLY RELIQUARY

The stern, hawk-nosed features of a tall priest looked down upon them with faint disapproval. "And what is it that has prompted you to ring our doorbell?"

"You're a bookstore, aren't you?" Vexx asked, pointing at his charred book. "We've got a book I think you might be interested in."

"We're more than just a mere bookstore," the priest said, unmoving, still blocking the entrance. "We are a holy reliquary. Though we do, indeed, host quite a collection of religious texts and magical tomes. Is this book of a holy or magical nature?"

"Right, right, that's what I meant. And this is as magical as it gets," Vexx said, opening the book. "See how my hair starts to rise? Pretty cool, right?"

The priest sighed and begrudgingly stepped back a few paces before frowning at Kaylin. "An elf. You two are not...involved, are you?"

"Oh, no," Vexx said with a pained smile.

After a moment, the priest stepped away, turning and

waving them over with a curt gesture. "Come in, I suppose. Follow me. Don't touch anything."

"Not yet, anyway," Vexx muttered, glancing at Kaylin as she walked past. *She isn't exactly my type, but we've been through a good deal together already. A hot elf like her?* He grinned at the idea, then smoothed his features, joining the solemn priest as he walked down the corridor.

"I didn't realize the church had such a powerful presence in Cloudbury."

"The Arch Rector does indeed grace this small town with his visits from time to time. I doubt he would approve of unwashed adventurers within these sacred walls."

Vexx bit back a scathing retort and plastered on a bland expression. Beside him, Kaylin frowned and discreetly sniffed at her hair. "Unwashed?" she muttered to herself.

"We have quite a large library of texts here," the tall priest said, as he turned left and opened a huge wooden door. "Brother Parneus! These visitors may have something of value."

"Oh, yes?"

Seated beside a map, a gray-haired monk blinked up at them, half-rising from his chair. The room was surrounded by sturdy wooden shelves, no doubt felled in the Lifeless Hills and fashioned in the nearby lumber mills. Their contents, on the other hand, were much more foreign. A grimoire surrounded with metal chains glowed a faint yellow, seeming to float in place, and beside it was a collection of leather-bound scrolls. The other shelves contained an enormous quantity of books, as well as a few curios and relics, a gleaming golden dragon's claw most prominent among them.

"I think you'll be very interested in this, sir," Vexx said, handing the book over, but the monk just frowned. He stared at Vexx for a long moment, as if attempting to solve a puzzle.

"You…you're the White boy, aren't you?" the monk asked after a moment.

Vexx flushed. "It's Vexx White, sir."

"Ah, I knew your father. Didn't much care for him. You…you were sent to the magical academy as a boy, weren't you?" The monk squinted. "But you were kicked out. I see you had your father's discipline."

"Hey! They just…" Vexx grimaced and gave up trying to explain himself. "Look, let's get this deal done and we'll be on our way."

"Fine," the monk said, opening the book. He skimmed through the first few pages. Then, his eyes widened as the hair on his fringe rose into the air. "This… this really is magic!"

"Told you."

He flipped to another page and a look of dismay descended upon his face. "Oh…oh no. Oh no."

Vexx frowned. "What?"

"Gaius, come here," the monk said to the tall priest, who hurried close and blanched as he looked at the pages. The monk continued skimming before finally slamming it closed and setting it on the table. He took a deep, shuddering breath.

"What's going on?" Vexx demanded.

"It's been profaned with demonic symbols. There is absolutely no way we could have this in our collection."

"I'll destroy it," Gaius announced, placing a hand on the book. Vexx rose to his feet, and to his surprise, Kaylin rose along with him, even taking a step forward to block the priest.

"That's our book!" she snapped.

"Damn straight," Vexx replied, earning glares from the others. But he was past caring now. "You want to destroy it? Well, you'll have to pay for it."

"I am not paying a single copper coin for those heretical ramblings," Gaius said even as he retracted his hand from the book. "It must be destroyed!"

"Heresy, is it?" Vexx glanced at the monk, who was shaking slightly from fear. "What does it say?"

"Nonsense," the monk stammered. "Ramblings about sacrifice and some Ruby of the Pure hidden in the Western Ruins! No, Gaius is right, it must be destroyed."

"Ruins…" Vexx muttered, then snatched up the book. "Fine, you won't pay? Then I'll destroy it myself."

"See that you do," Gaius said with a slight look of fear in his eyes. "There is foul magic trapped inside."

The sensation of magic kept barely at bay travelled up Vexx's arm. But it seemed familiar by now, and the discomfort lessened as he dropped it into his leather pack.

"Don't worry yourselves. I'll take care of it."

Gaius grunted and quickly ushered them out of the room. "See that you do. I will see you out."

Kaylin paused for a moment. "Do you have a restroom I can use?"

"We do not have restrooms, for the truly devout never rest, but we do have a washroom."

"Over here?" Kaylin asked, pointing towards a massive white door with a shimmering golden doorknob.

"No! We keep our most priceless artifacts in there. Holy relics, fashioned by master goldsmiths. Not for the likes of you to see." The priest jerked his head to the left. "The washroom is over there."

20

CARAVAN GUARDS

"Your church officials are a very cranky bunch," Kaylin observed once they had left the reliquary.

"Yeah, I never much cared for them," Vexx replied. "Too many rules for my tastes."

"So, what do you want to do after we destroy the book?" Kaylin asked. "Maybe we could find someone else who needs a dungeon cleared."

"You heard what they said," Vexx replied. "The Western Ruins? I think I know which ones they meant. The old empire used to have a garrison here centuries ago, though it's been abandoned for ages. I've heard there are wights and spirits that haunt it to this day."

"If there are wights, maybe you could say you're family, Vexx!"

Vexx White kept his face carefully neutral. "Don't. Just…don't." He raised the scroll up high.

"Get it?" Kaylin grinned guilelessly. "Because—"

"Let's get ourselves something to eat," Vexx snapped. "I've got to plan our next adventure."

❧

A HALF HOUR later found Vexx idly munching on a loaf of bread. Food had given him a clearer picture of the adventure. He unrolled a cheap map and tapped it with the end of his dagger as Kaylin looked on, midway through her meal of noodles in some sort of strange sauce.

"So, we're here in Cloudbury. We'll have to skirt the Lifeless Hills, but there's a logging road heading northwest, and if we're lucky, we might be able to earn a few coins as caravan guards on that route. Lots of goblin raids, or so I hear. Now…" Vexx moved his dagger and tapped an image of a ruined castle. "We'll go off the road and head south. The old Imperial ruins are here. The caravans avoid it, so we'll have to travel alone at that point. Based on what I've gathered in the dead adventurer's scroll and the magic book, I'm fairly confident the Ruby of the Pure can be found there."

Kaylin slurped up her noodles and nodded. "How do you know which way's northwest?"

"Magic."

"Oooh…"

They paused as a woman in farmer's garb passed by, watching as she shuffled through the cramped outdoor eating area. It was packed full for the mid-day meal, a crowd that consisted of loggers and shopkeepers eating simple fare from overworked stalls. A few hunters, often wearing their own pelts, could be found around the periphery and there were about a dozen farmers and ranchers taking a break from the errands that had brought them to Cloudbury.

No strangers though, and no elves in this crowd —certainly none as attractive as Kaylin.

Vexx had seen more than a few looks at Kaylin, though she seemed cheerfully unaware of it, and Vexx himself had even been the subject of a few stares as well.

We stick out here, even though I grew up just outside town. Well, so what? We're dungeoneers now, and they are just common folk.

Vexx straightened up before he carefully rolled up the map and placed it in his leather satchel beside the adventurer's scroll and the magical book—which still seemed to hum with energy. "I think it's about time we got out of here," Vexx said. "Let's make for the Western Gate and see if there's a caravaneer in need of protection."

Kaylin leaned back, setting her empty bowl on the table. "But why, Vexx?"

"Why?" Vexx blinked. "To find this ruby! You think something like that won't sell? Hells, we might be rich at the end of this adventure! That's real dungeoneering, it is. Besides, do you have any better ideas?"

Kaylin thought for a moment. "Nope!"

❧

It wasn't long before they met a merchant at the Western Gate looking for protection. He was no caravan leader, with only a single horse-drawn wagon loaded down with pelts, but he was looking for protection and they were looking for work.

"It's a rough country up ahead," he said, eyeing them with thinly-veiled skepticism. "I'll only be hiring you for a half day's work—once we pass the Lifeless Hills, I'll go the rest of the way alone and sell my goods at the port. And to be honest with you, a scrawny kid and an elf girl don't look too intimidating."

"Hey!" Vexx frowned, snapping his fingers, and a ball of fire emerged to float around it. "We can handle ourselves."

"That's right!" Kaylin said with a resolute nod. "We often handle ourselves!"

The merchant blinked in bewilderment. "Well…just don't do that on the job. Alright, three coppers each when we make it past the Lifeless Hills. I'm in a hurry. Frank's my regular guard while in Cloudbury, and he's used to working with freelancers on these trips."

This "Frank" character stepped forward from the other side of the wagon. He was a tall man approaching middle age, with dark, balding hair and a scruffy beard. There was a long scar along his forehead and his huge double-headed axe was slung casually over his shoulder. His outfit was a mix of wolf hide and boiled leather, though the sleeves appeared to have been cut off as it to show off his muscular arms. His lips spread as he attempted either a grimace or a friendly smile—it was hard to be sure.

"Hey, you two, the name's Frank. Haven't seen either of you before. Have you done any caravan guarding work?"

"What's a caravan?" Kaylin asked.

Frank frowned and scratched at his stubble. "So that's how this is gonna be," he muttered to himself.

"We have some dungeoneering experience," Vexx said. "We've killed our share of goblins."

Frank grunted. "Well, this is a small operation. Not even a caravan, really, just a single merchant. Unfortunately, the goblins love little groups like this. I've seen them let bands of twenty horsemen and logging carts go right on by and swoop down on a couple stragglers just a minute later." He shrugged. "They're sneaky bastards, so keep your weapons ready."

"I don't need a weapon," Vexx said confidently. "I have my magic."

"You're a mage?" Frank raised an eyebrow. "Don't get too many of your kind as guards, though I suppose a healer is always handy."

"Not a healer," Vexx snapped. "Or...a mage either, technically. I don't have my diploma, I mean. But who needs it?"

"Mages, probably," Frank said with a shrug. "But I ain't exactly the academy type so it doesn't mean a damn thing to me. Just kill goblins if they attack, alright? I don't much care how you do it."

"Got it."

Frank turned to look at the merchant, who was patting his horse and saying a few calming words. The wagon was pulled by a huge plow horse, and while Vexx doubted it could go much over walking pace, it seemed the perfect choice for eating up the miles between scattered towns.

"We're ready, boss!"

The merchant nodded, taking his seat on the wagon, and spurred his horse onward. The wagon lurched forward, rumbling as it rattled against the cobblestones. Vexx and Kaylin fell into position on the left and right while Frank hurried up to scout a dozen paces ahead of the wagon.

"Keep your eyes sharp, guards!" the merchant said as they passed the Western Gate, the spearmen stationed beside it nodding their heads in bored recognition. "And your weapons ready!"

21

AMBUSH

The wagon trundled along, a monotonous rumble that filled the silence as Vexx continually scanned the nearby forest that flanked the southern side of the road. The ground dipped down, littered with scattered boulders and twisted corpses of trees, though it was a steep slope on the northern side. *Kaylin will be watching that side. Even though she's the clumsiest elf I've ever met, she's always been good at spotting things.*

They were midway through the pass that went across a dip in the ridgeline of the Lifeless Hills, and they had yet to see any sign of either goblins or traffic. *Aside from that abandoned cart a while back, with the shallow graves beside it.* Vexx scanned back and forth, back and forth. *Still, we're making good progress, and it seems like we won't run into any—*

"Goblins!"

The shout came from Kaylin on the other side of the wagon, followed an instant later by the thrum of her bow.

"Vexx! Over here!" she called out.

At the same moment, there came a string of curses

from the wagon, and Vexx turned before quickly hurrying to the other side. He glanced up to see a swarm of charging goblins, just as Kaylin loosed her first arrow. A goblin took the hit full in the chest and tumbled down the slope. The other goblins roared as they charged down, trampling their fallen comrade. Flames appeared beside Vexx's outstretched hands, and he quickly launched fireball after fireball.

He heard a twang nearby and saw a crossbow bolt sail out, followed by the merchant cursing and furiously winching to reload. Vexx heard the distant bellow of Frank charging from the front, but spared no time to watch the barbarian, instead setting the slope ablaze with a curtain of fire. Dark figures emerged from behind the curtain of fire, streaming forward with upraised weapons and shrill cries. Vexx felt spent from the magic but sent a final burst of flames to keep them at bay.

Vexx sank to his knees, glancing up even as he fumbled in his satchel. He swore and cursed his stamina as he watched the goblins charge forward. He raised the half-full potion to his lips before ripping the cork out and spitting it to the side, drinking it thirstily before tossing the empty vial to the ground. Vexx rose on unsteady legs, already feeling the energy returning to him, then dodged aside as a goblin's axe slashed just where he had been a moment before.

Vexx slammed the goblin with a fireball, sending the charred and screaming creature flying into the air, then whirled and fired three quick fireballs at the remaining goblins in the area. He heard shouts and the clatter of combat nearby but kept his focus on everything around him. His head throbbed dimly as the final smoldering goblin collapsed to the ground beside the road. A few others were fleeing back up the slope, one collapsing to its knees as Kaylin's arrow pierced through its shoulder. Further to his right, Vexx looked on as Frank roared in exultation, grinning fiercely as he decapitated a goblin with his gigantic axe.

Vexx let out a long breath and felt a sense of achievement growing within him, as if that last fight had been some marker of a boost in experience.

What a rush!

Frank's hearty laugh caught his attention, and Vexx looked over to see the barbarian approaching, his bloody axe resting on one shoulder. "Nice shooting, elf!" he called out, nodding at Kaylin as she lowered her bow. "You too, kiddo," he added to Vexx, raising an eyebrow at a still-burning goblin corpse.

"It's Vexx White," he replied in annoyance. "Soon, they'll be talking about me just like Dred Wyrm. Mark my words."

Frank smirked but said nothing.

"You, guards!" the merchant called out, standing atop his wagon with his crossbow still in hand. "Any wounds?"

The three of them confirmed they were unscathed and the merchant nodded, pleased. "Good work! I'll give you a few minutes to loot the corpses, if you'd like, and then we'll be on our way. I doubt they'd be foolish enough to attack us again."

The guards spread out, picking over the remains, Vexx gingerly patted at the charred corpse of a goblin. He was rewarded with a few stinking coppers. *Everything helps, I suppose.* Vexx had checked a few of the bodies, and now approached one with an arrow in the heart. *Not my kill, but at least it doesn't smell like a rotten barbeque.* He yanked the arrow out to give back to Kaylin.

My fireballs are pretty effective, Vexx thought as he eyed the corpse, *but my bursts of flames are too exhausting to use that often. I don't need to improve them just yet, but with my newfound experience…what if I tried reanimating the body?* He had communed with spirits before; the ghosts that haunted the cemetery attached to the magical academy. This was a step beyond, but…

But I've trained hard enough that it should be possible now.

He extended his hand, feeling the glow of his new experience fade away, flickering green magic pulsing out of his hand and into the dead goblin. The faded eyes of the goblin glowed a demonic red, the creature's left arm shifted and its dirty fingers dug into the ground as the creature struggled to rise to its feet.

Vexx felt a rush of excitement, a dim sense of another creature at his command, an undead minion to—

"Time to go!" the merchant shouted. "I have a schedule to keep!"

Vexx released his control, the light dying again in the goblin's eyes, the creature falling motionless once more. *I'll save that trick for later. Besides, the others might freak out about it.*

"Vexx!"

"Coming!" he replied, hurrying back to the wagon, smiling all the while.

22

TO THE RUINS

"You've done good work for me," the merchant said, his plow horse peacefully grazing at a patch of grass just off the road. They had passed the last of the Lifeless Hills some ways back and were in open country now. It was a peaceful land here, or as peaceful as anything got. "Look me up next time I'm in Cloudbury," he said, tossing three small cloth bags at his guards, weighted down with coins.

Frank caught one, Vexx caught one, and the third smacked into Kaylin's face.

"Ow!" she muttered.

The merchant frowned. "You, I'm not so sure about. Anyway, until next time," he said, spurring his horse forward. Kaylin bent down and picked up her coin purse as the wagon rumbled away from its former guards.

"Good work, newbies," Frank said. "I'll travel back to Cloudbury with you if you're going that way."

"We're not *that* new," Vexx protested. "We're not going back to Cloudbury just yet, anyway. You'll be on your own."

"Oh?" Frank raised his eyebrows. "I don't mind; I'm just surprised. Are you raiding a dungeon out here?" He paused for a moment. "Ah, well, I won't pry. I'm not trying to interfere with your quest. Best of luck to the two of you!"

"Actually…"

Vexx looked over at Kaylin. She had been counting her coins but dropped one into the dusty road. "Three, four… shit! Where was I…"

"You know, we could use another fighter."

Frank eyed them for a moment and pensively scratched at his scruffy beard. "I can see that. Given that you're newbies, I would normally charge more for babysitting, but I can see that you have a lead on some treasure. I'm in for a third of the reward."

Vexx fixed him with a level stare, letting the insult about babysitting wash over him. *There could be a serious fight up ahead, and at least we know this guy can handle himself.* "We do. It's called the Ruby of the Pure. We can do a third once we sell it."

"Nuh-uh," Kaylin cut in, shaking her head. "That doesn't sound fair. We should do it fifty-fifty-fifty. Tell him, Vexx!"

Vexx breathed out deliberately and prayed for patience. "Right…sure. Like the lady says. Fifty-fifty-fifty."

Frank smirked. "She drives a hard bargain, but I can work with that. Where are we headed?"

"The ruins of the old Imperial garrison south of here. I have good information on this one."

Frank nodded slowly. "I've heard stories about that place. It won't be too easy. And it'll be night by the time we get there." He breathed out slowly. "Ghosts and spirits at night?" He shrugged. "Well, no time like the present. Lead on, wizard."

⁂

FRANK AND VEXX stood in the silence beside an ancient, half-collapsed chapel on the outskirts of the ruined garrison. They had taken a look inside the ancient chapel, but it had been picked over ages ago. Now they waited near a gap in the broken-down stone wall that ringed the ruins. Kaylin had slipped in to scout a path for them some time ago, but they had heard nothing since then.

"So, you and Kaylin," Frank began, then fell silent.

"Yeah?"

"Are you two…you know. An item."

"Ah…well, no."

"I see…"

The silence lingered.

"So you wouldn't mind if I asked—"

A hiss interrupted them and they looked over as a shadowy figure emerged from over the sloping wall. It waved its hand and a moment later, Vexx recognized her as Kaylin. She had evidently found a good way in. Vexx crept forward, Frank following closely behind.

"Like I was saying," he whispered, "you wouldn't mind—"

"Let's just focus on the mission," Vexx replied, irritated now. *Do I mind?* He caught a glimpse of Kaylin, her easy smile and smooth skin looking especially beautiful in the moonlight. Vexx smiled in return as he took position beside her, shifting his shoulder in front of Frank.

"The stories about ghosts don't appear to be true," Kaylin said in a soft voice.

"Or you can't see them," Frank said over Vexx's shoulder. Vexx shifted over more to block Kaylin's view of him.

"Did you find the General's Headquarters? The Ruby of the Pure is said to be kept in a treasure chest inside."

"Yes, but I kept my distance. I don't want to trigger any traps or anything."

Frank peeked his head around. "You're as wise as you are beau—"

"Let's go, then!" Vexx snapped, already rising to his feet. "Frank, circle around the left. Kaylin and I will go around from the right."

Frank looked like he was about to argue, but after a moment, he nodded. "Fine."

Keeping light on their feet, Vexx and Kaylin prowled through the empty dirt alleys, trash and debris that must have fallen centuries ago littered on the ground. There was no saying exactly why these outposts had fallen all that time ago. Vexx supposed it must have once had Imperial relics before other dungeoneers had carted them out.

Still, the Ruby of the Pure should still be there. I hope.

"I'm glad we have Frank with us," Kaylin said after a moment. Her alert eyes scanned for threats as they walked. They were in an open field leading to the General's Headquarters, with just a couple ruined buildings marring the landscape.

"Are you?" Vexx asked, surprised at the unexpected bitterness in his words.

"Yeah! He seems nice."

"He's not that nice," Vexx muttered, passing through the end of the alley. "I've been thinking. Three is a terrible number for having adventures. Maybe after this, we can go back to just the two of us. We could get a nice dinner together from the loot and—"

"Hey, Vexx?"

"Uh, yeah?"

Kaylin had paused, pointing at a glowing symbol, a magical ward mostly concealed by a bush. Vexx whistled at the sight. That was a cunning trap, and they had almost walked into it. An ancient Imperial flagon gleamed in the moonlight, the pristine silver and masterful etchings made a perfect lure for looters.

"You were right to wait for me. That's a magic ward," Vexx pointed out. "You see the glowing symbol? It's triggered by the central axis, which is right below that flagon there. It uses pressure on that point to turn off and on."

"You're so smart!"

Vexx grinned. "I was taught the basic principles at the magical academy, but it wasn't something I specialized in."

"Ah…" Kaylin nodded. "So if you just touch this one…" Before Vexx could say anything, Kaylin pressed the indicated symbol. It flashed red for a moment and then disappeared. Vexx saw flashes of red in the distance. Kaylin looked over and smiled. "That turns it off?"

Vexx gritted his teeth. "No."

The ground rumbled below them and a skeletal hand shot out of the ground. Then another, and another. Vexx grabbed Kaylin by the arm and pointed at the headquarters building. "Run!"

23

THE IMPERIAL GARRISON

Unearthly howls echoed all around the previously abandoned Imperial garrison. A dark figure emerged from a nearby ruin and Vexx almost let out an undignified scream at the sight before he realized it was Frank. Vexx caught other flashes of movement in the distance and ran even faster.

"What happened?" Frank asked, joining with them as they sprinted to the headquarters building.

"You must have triggered a ward," Vexx said in between breaths.

"To the right!" Kaylin shouted.

Vexx glanced right, eyes roving over a squad of skeleton warriors marching in formation. The clattering of their bones mixed in with the dull clangs of swords, and as they drew closer, Vexx could smell the musk of their rotting wooden shields. Kaylin loosed a quick arrow, which embedded itself into one of their skulls, but didn't appear to slow the skeleton warrior down at all. Vexx flung fireball after fireball, but there didn't seem to be an end to them, and he rejoined the others as they reached the square outside the headquarters building.

It was already filling with more skeleton warriors.

The others had demolished a squad of skeleton warriors up close, the enemies deceptively fragile when it came to melee attacks. Frank grimaced, panting as he swiped a finger over the side of his head, cursing as a thin trail of blood dripped dangerously near his eye.

"We'll charge our way through!" Frank shouted as he ran forward, grunting as he swept a skeleton warrior off its feet with a low strike. "And barricade the door! With me!"

"Are you sure?" Vexx asked, then saw that waves of skeleton warriors were approaching from both sides. "Ah, dammit! Kaylin, let's go!"

Kaylin had strapped her bow to her back some time ago and was wildly swinging an ancient mace and a rusted sword, both of which she had picked up from fallen skeleton warriors. Another crumbled to pieces before her. Clumsy as she was, with weapons in both hands, it seemed she could hardly miss.

Side by side, they stormed forward, catching up to Frank. He was barreling through a squad when one of them sliced into his left arm. Vexx blew it to bits with a fireball as Frank struggled forward, taking another stab before Kaylin batted it away with her dual weapons.

"For...ward," Frank coughed as he continued to swing his axe. He landed heavy blows on a persistent skeleton as he cleared a way through, fighting his way up the steps toward the General's Headquarters. A flurry of arrows flew over them as they stormed ahead. Vexx gritted his teeth, wishing he had the strength and money to afford platemail. His robe would be useless against those arrows, and its poison effect wouldn't do a thing to the undead.

"We're almost there!" Kaylin cried out.

Vexx had turned around, the rear guard now, blasting fireballs at the closest pursuers. "There's no end to them!" A few of them were archers, loosing arrows that passed just barely overhead, and Vexx favored them with a huge fireball even as he felt his energy draining.

There was a loud splintering of ancient wood as Frank burst through the door ahead. Kaylin and Vexx followed close behind as the barbarian staggered to the floor, spattering the dusty flagstones with his blood. *At least there's nothing inside—except for a treasure chest! But there's no time for that now.*

Vexx and Kaylin braced themselves at the door, guarding the narrow entrance.

"Ah, shit!" Frank yelled. "Healer! I need a heal!"

"Who are you talking to?" Vexx asked, pausing between throwing fireballs. "I can't heal you!"

"Ugh…" Frank rasped out as he sunk to a knee, batting ineffectually at one of the arrows sticking out from his body. "This…went…" he coughed. "Poorly."

"On the left!" Kaylin called out, swinging her rusted sword at an approaching skeleton warrior and shattering its skull. The broken bones of a wave of skeleton warriors coated the stairs and empty square outside. But not far away, another marching formation of skeleton warriors was approaching. Vexx slammed the battered door shut, for whatever good that would do.

"Isn't there anything you can do for him?" Kaylin asked, crouching beside Frank. "Anything at all?"

"No," Vexx said in a low voice, watching as the life faded from Frank's eyes. "At least…not yet."

24

THE RUBY OF THE PURE

Vexx wiped sweat off his brow, then raised his hand over the fresh corpse of Frank. Green tendrils of spectral energy flickered down to the fallen barbarian. Kaylin blanched. "I'll check on the treasure," she said, before quickly moving away. Vexx swayed from exhaustion, but kept his focus, staring down at Frank.

Come on, come on!

Frank's eyes flicked open, his hazel brown eyes bleeding to a glowing green, and he rumbled something unintelligible.

"Get up, Frank!" Vexx snapped. "Hold that door."

"Mmm…" Frank moaned as he shakily got to his feet, his movements sluggish. "Kay…lin…" he said slowly, as if unfamiliar with language..

"Hold the door, Frank!" Vexx commanded, sending the symbol through. The door rocked with a sudden impact. *The skeleton warriors are just about to bash it open.* Zombie Frank stood still for a long moment, then lurched toward the door, hefting his battle-axe. Vexx turned to see

Kaylin approaching with a red orb in one hand and a rusted sword in the other.

"Poor Frank! Well, I guess it's just fifty-fifty now," Kaylin said, holding the Ruby of the Pure up high. "Unless zombies get a cut."

Vexx grunted, fishing for a mana potion. "Anything else in there?" he asked, popping the cork.

"That's it," Kaylin said. "We got what we came for, but…"

Vexx chugged the potion, wiping his mouth with his sleeve, and threw the empty glass bottle to shatter on the floor. He didn't say it out loud, but he knew what she was thinking.

But we're trapped in here. Nine out of ten dungeoneers don't make it past their first ten quests. And here we are at number three.

"Let's see, let's see…" Vexx rummaged through his leather satchel, trying to calm himself and think of a way out. *I'm almost out of potions, and I don't have…*

Vexx blinked, feeling the familiar surge of magic as he touched the book. *The book. Of course! I was going to try the ritual later, but…the book does hold great power within it!* A smash interrupted his thoughts and Vexx glanced over to see the door broken open. Zombie Frank lurched in, slower than usual, but strong enough to smash the skulls of the two closest skeletons.

"Vexx, do you have a plan?" Kaylin stammered.

"Yeah, yeah, one second," he replied, skimming through the book. "Great power…a trap…should not be unleashed…some demon symbols…all good so far."

Zombie Frank was still holding position at the door, scattering the bones of a skeleton warrior that was a half-second too late. An arrow soared past, taking Zombie

Frank in his right leg, though he had no reaction to it. Another followed, and then a skeleton with a mace trudged up the stairs.

"He can't hold forever! What can we do?"

"Uh... " Vexx frantically flipped through the last pages of the magic book. "Yeah, here it is! Feed magic into the Ruby of the Pure while holding a lock of hair from the innocent. Hey!" He looked over at Kaylin. "You're pretty innocent, right?"

She blinked. "Of what?" she asked innocently.

Vexx leaned over and plucked a hair from her. Kaylin yelped. Vexx ignored her, grabbing the Ruby of the Pure from her hands. With the hair and ruby clenched tightly in both hands Vexx closed his eyes and concentrated, feeding magical energy into the orb. *It's now or never!*

He felt heat rising in both hands and opened his eyes. The book had fallen on the ground below and the pages rustled, moving back and forth as a wave of wind and energy stirred from within. The book began to hover in the air, vibrating rapidly, and Vexx felt a sudden coolness in his palms. He opened both hands and watched in horrified fascination as black ashes trailed out from where the ruby had been and blackened hair fibers drifted down from his open right hand.

Something has gone wrong!

"Am I...cursed?" Vexx asked in shock, staring at a black mark left on his left palm where the ruby had been. He rubbed at it furiously with the fingers on his right hand, ignoring the sounds of struggle at the door, watching as bits of ashes drifted away, but the mark remained. "Oh, this isn't good. This isn't good at all. How innocent are you, really?"

"What do you mean?"

"Ah, you know these old books! They always mean virgin when they say innocent."

"Ohhh…" Kaylin replied slowly. "Why didn't you say so before?" They looked at each other in silence for a long moment.

"Well?" Vexx asked over the commotion at the door. "A lady doesn't kiss and tell."

Before Vexx could reply, the swirling magical book burst apart and flashes of black and red blinded him.

"Yeah, somebody let me out!" a woman's voice declared triumphantly.

A spectral form appeared as the multicolored haze faded away, and then, a half-naked woman materialized. Form-fitting mesh covered parts of her body but did nothing to hide her ample curves. She hovered in the air for a moment; long black hair mixed with red, and she fixed her eyes on Vexx with a wide smile.

"What an attractive young man! I see these centuries weren't wasted. I mean, they were, but here we are."

"Wha…" Vexx stammered. "You… you're…"

"Shy," the strange woman said. Judging from her tight clothing, it didn't seem likely. "That's my nickname, anyway. My full name is Shyola." She set her hands on her hips and studied him. "Oh, you'll be a delight. I'll save you for later. You, on the other hand…" Shy shrugged as she looked over to Kaylin, and in a flash, she drew a whip. She cackled as she flicked her wrist and it snapped forward to circle around Kaylin.

Kaylin shrieked and desperately struggled against the pulsating orange magic that surged through the whip.

Shyola grinned, licked her lips. "Sacrifices are lacking these days, but—"

Vexx whipped his hand forward, sending his magic straight toward Shyola's head, using his new necromantic skill. *She isn't a corpse, but she isn't exactly "alive"…is she?* He strained, rapidly draining his energy reserves in an attempt to make her submit. Vexx's eyes flicked past Shy, who now moved away in surprise, over to Zombie Frank still holding the door against an attacking wave.

"Frank!" Vexx snapped, still struggling to control the demon. "Help!"

Something smashed in the distance. "Frank bus—" another smash sound. "Busy. No time for—" he paused, and another smash echoed over. "Play."

Vexx groaned. He supposed his zombie had a point, but still. He glared at Shyola. "Yield to me, demon!"

Shy staggered and fell to her knees. "I don't know if it's," she panted, "centuries of lounging around in there, or…" she shook her head. "Or what, but…" Shy groaned and released her whip, the magical cord disappearing around Kaylin.

"You got me," Shy said, grinning even as she slumped forward. "You got me," she said again, sighing heavily before rising to her feet "Alright, I'm bound to you, Master. You have three wishes."

"Wait…you're a genie?"

She laughed. "No, I've just been waiting for so long to make that joke. I'm a succubus! That means—"

She disappeared in a puff of red light, and then reappeared right behind Vexx, whispering into his ear, "Whatever you want it to mean, Master."

Vexx stumbled away in surprise and crashed into Kaylin. *I am so uncomfortably aroused right now.* He glanced up as Zombie Frank collapsed under the surging attacks of three skeleton warriors. The spectral green energy flickered and faded around him and the empty white eye sockets of the skeleton warriors fixed themselves on them.

"Uh, I wish…I wish for them to go away!"

The succubus sighed. "Like I said, darling, I'm not a genie. But as you wish," she said, flicking a spectral whip that flashed into existence. She slashed it at the skeleton warriors, severing them in half. "There will be more coming, Master. They will never. Stop. Coming."

Vexx licked his lips. "We need to get out of here."

"Ah, so young and insightful! We will have a good lifetime, Master. Wait. Who's this bitch?"

Kaylin smiled weakly and extended a hand. "Kaylin Lulynn, Miss Shy. What's it like to be in a book?"

Shy sniffed disdainfully. "You get used to it. Master, can I kill her?"

"What? No," Vexx said, scanning the room for exits. More skeleton warriors were emerging from the entrance, trampling the doubly lifeless corpse of Zombie Frank. "Shit, shit!"

"Never fear, Master. When one door closes," she paused to flick her whip above the skeleton warriors, searing through the masonry above and sending the ancient stone collapsing down onto the skeletons. "Another…opens!" she screamed out as she fired a burst of magic into the nearby wall, flinging huge blocks of stone into the night. The new entrance yawned open, but the entire building shook unsteadily, bits of dust and debris fell around them as the room started collapsing.

"Let's go!" Shy shouted, spanking Vexx with her enhanced energy and sending him flying through the entrance. Vexx sprawled on the grass outside and staggered to his feet. He looked over to see the succubus sauntering calmly out of the hole in the wall. The building was collapsing around her, though she didn't even bother to look back. A second later, Kaylin leaped through the entrance and barely made it onto the grass outside. She swayed where she stood before dropping in a heap beside Vexx.

Shy frowned down at her. "Still alive, I see," she said. "A shame."

"You two," Vexx said as he rose to his feet. "Need to get along. But right now?" He looked over to see spectral forms materializing as they streamed out of nearby ruins, their translucent, blue-tinted forms hefted warhammers and battle-axes. "Let's get out of here!"

26

THE GENERAL'S MAUSOLEUM

E very time they turned a corner in the ruins, they found themselves hemmed in; whether by glowing, malevolent spirits or by roving squads of skeleton warriors. Shy slashed one of these squads with her whip, turning back to look at Vexx, who dispelled the circling orb of fire he'd readied.

"I'm afraid we're surrounded, Master. The elf's fault, I would assume."

"Somewhat," Vexx muttered, glancing over at Kaylin. She had run over to an ornate marble building that was supported by cracked pillars. *A decent place for a final stand, I suppose. So much for being the next Dred Wyrm.*

"You can't teleport us out, can you?"

"Unfortunately not," she replied. "If I die in this world, I'll be transported back to one of the hells. I don't particularly mind it, but I would hate to lose you, darling, when we have only just met."

"I imagine I'll join you soon," Vexx replied, glancing at a swarm of ghosts circling above, evidently keeping tabs on their movements.

"It won't be the same one," Shy said in a disappointed voice. "You'd need several human lifetimes to commit the number of sins that would earn you a place in mine."

"Vexx, over here!"

He looked over to see Kaylin waving from behind the pillar. Vexx gritted his teeth and ran over with Shy in tow.

"Oh, I recognize this," Shy said as she approached. "This is General Pel-Kantheon's mausoleum. He died in the wars shortly before I was trapped, actually. Highly renowned, *highly*. They used to say his legion would follow him into all the hells. Kind of cute, too, if I remember correctly."

"Really…" Vexx mused.

"I mean, if you're into that. Close-cropped jaw, full lips…he was balding, but it added a certain gravitas to his—"

"Not that," Vexx snapped, putting his shoulder on the sarcophagus's lid. "Help me get this off!"

Kaylin joined him without question, straining at the heavy marble, which started to give. Shy, on the other hand, just whistled in amusement.

"Really, you're that interested? And with danger on all sides? You're twisted, Master, much more twisted than I'd imagine. And I'm very imagin—"

"Shut up and help me!"

Shy joined them, and the lid slid further away, opening a wide gap. Then, it fell to the ground on the other side with a heavy thunk. Vexx stood up and looked down at the linen-wrapped corpse of General Pel-Kantheon.

"This won't do," he muttered, tearing at the linens and exposing the corpse's ancient face. "Shy, help me get it up!"

The succubus let out a long sigh. "I'm normally quite good at that, but—"

"Kaylin!"

Kaylin and Vexx grabbed the corpse of the general and together, they hauled him out of the mausoleum. Shy simply looked on in confusion. Together, Vexx and Kaylin set him against the wall at the entrance. Vexx glanced over to see a veritable horde of skeletons and spirits approaching.

This had better work.

Vexx extended his right hand, green spectral energy flowing toward and around the linen-wrapped corpse. Beside him, Kaylin half-raised her bow, but hesitated. Arrows were next to useless against a single skeleton warrior, not to mention a whole legion, and he knew she didn't have many left.

"Good luck, Vexx," she whispered.

A moment passed, then another, and Vexx grimaced as he braced for the swords of a legion of skeleton warriors to plunge into him. But then—a faint green light appeared in one eye socket, and then lit up in the other one. The corpse general lurched to the side and strained against its wrappings before looking down as if surprised to find itself trapped in them.

"Stop them," Vexx said in a faint voice, half desperate whisper, half command. The ancient, weathered face looked at him for a long moment. Then it nodded and turned towards the approaching horde. Vexx stepped back a few paces, Shy and Kaylin kept close on both sides as if for protection.

"I didn't realize you were a necromancer!" Shy said, her eyebrows raised.

"Haaauuwt…" the corpse general rasped, its ancient, rotting jaw twitching. "Haaahhhh…tuh."

The charging skeleton warriors slowed. Then, they came to an uncertain halt. One of them stood stiff and twitched, its right arm slowly rising. The finger bones tapped against its skull and it remained there; rigid and motionless. Then another skeleton warrior mimicked the motion, then another, and another. The spirits slowed, hovering above the skeleton warriors, and then dispersed to various gaps in what appeared to be a growing formation.

"Staaaaah…undah. Ah. Tennn…shun."

As one, the skeletons straightened, but Vexx wasn't there to see it. Instead, he was crouched behind Shyola, trying his best not to be distracted by her shapely butt as Kaylin led the three of them to creep away through the back. *I swear she's wiggling it on purpose.* They proceeded in silence until they reached the gap in the wall.

"Amazing," Kaylin muttered as she glanced back.

"Well, the Imperial legion was supposed to be well-trained, after all," Vexx said in a low voice as they clambered over stones and debris. "Now, then. We'll need to get at least a mile away from here before we can make camp. I'm going to have nightmares as it is."

"I can help you relax," Shy said seductively as they bounded away into the darkness.

"Ahhh…eash!" came the distant rasp of the corpse general, followed by a rattle of bones. "Baaahhh…to… yo…gwaves!"

27

THE SUCCUBUS AND THE SACRIFICE

"Help! Vexx!"

Vexx's eyes flicked open and he groaned. He had only just managed to get to sleep and they were under attack already? Vexx staggered to his feet.

"What...what is it?" He blinked and looked over, confused at what he saw. Two figures struggled, and as Vexx came to his feet and cast his bleary eyes over to the commotion, he saw a couple of attractive, half-dressed women scuffling with each other.

Am I dreaming?

Vexx shook his head and blinked, now seeing that Shy had wrapped Kaylin with her whip, and was now keeping her firmly in place. Kaylin was once again bound in Shy's whip—though this time, the elf was just in her under-clothes. "Time to break my fast," Shy cackled, teeth bared.

"Don't even think about it!" Vexx roared, two fireballs already readied and circling around his fists. Shy just looked over in annoyance and disbelief.

"Master, really? Fighting me over this girl? Some time with me, and you won't miss her one bit."

"Let her go!"

The moment dragged on. Vexx flicked his gaze to the right at Kaylin, who was still squirming in her bindings. He flicked his eyes left to Shyola, who licked her lips, expression inscrutable. *She had been so close to throwing off my domination spell before. Would she try now?*

"How quick do you think you are with those fireballs, Master?" Shy asked.

Vexx didn't reply. Instead, he kept his fingers loose and flexible, his right fireball aimed at the whip holding Kaylin, the left facing Shyola directly. A cool wind blew, flickering his flames, and a stray weed tumbled between them as the standoff continued.

Finally, Shyola waved her hand in a careless gesture and vanished her whip. Without the whip holding her in place, Kaylin tumbled out of the air and fell to the ground in a disgruntled heap. Vexx breathed a sigh of relief and expelled his flames.

"I still need to apply my eyeshadow today," Shyola said in a flippant voice, "so I can wait on a meal for a little while. But I do need to suck her dry, Master. It was part of the contract."

"What contract?" Vexx scoffed. "I didn't sign any contract."

"It's in the book!" Shy pointed out. "I should know. I was in there for centuries."

"It said you need the hair of the innocent. Not their bodies...or souls, or whatever."

"Ah, clearly it's implied." Shyola crossed her arms and rolled her eyes. She looked back at him and blew a stray strand of hair out of her face "I mean, I hate to be a stickler for contracts, but if nothing else, it takes a lot of energy to travel across dimensions. I've got to drain some-body's life force."

Kaylin rose to her feet and made a face at Shyola before dusting off her knees. "I'm really starting to hate this demon, Vexx." She yawned. "I guess I'll get dressed."

Shy rolled her eyes. "You see how she flirts with you, Master?"

"Flirting? I'm just putting my clothes on!" Kaylin shouted back, already shrugging her top on. Vexx was finding it very difficult to avoid looking at her—and Shy wasn't much better, her outfit half mesh and half crisscrossing leather straps. He mustered the last dregs of his willpower and stared somewhere in between the two of them. At least he was awake now.

"So...you need to eat someone," Vexx stated slug-gishly. "Or something?"

"Not just eat. Devour their life force. It can't be dead yet, it needs to wriggle and writhe around..."

"So like a worm?"

Shy sighed. "Let's not start off like this, Master. You really don't want me to overpower this bond and suck *you* dry instead. Or..." she arched an eyebrow. "Maybe you do."

Vexx suddenly brightened. "I have an idea!"

"Oh?" Shy asked. "You *do* want that? Well, I can make it enjoyable, though you won't live through it." She smiled at Kaylin, who was adjusting her skirt. "And you'd be next."

"No," Vexx shook his head in exasperation. "I know what you can feed on. Come on, let's get started. We're all awake now, anyway."

The dungeoneers packed up quickly, and all the while, Vexx kept a close eye on both Shyola and Kaylin, and it wasn't long before they had set off on the winding road that led to Cloudbury.

"You are from here, Master?" Shyola asked as they plodded along.

"From Cloudbury? Well, yes. More or less."

"More or less?" Shy raised an eyebrow in curiosity, and even Kaylin looked over. It wasn't like they had talked much of the past, but Vexx found that he didn't mind. It helped him endure the long trek, at least.

"My mother and father met in Oerchenbrach. It's north of here, by the sea. I grew up there, actually, though I barely remember it at all. There was a plague, and…" Vexx trailed off, unexpected emotion surging through his chest. "Well, after my mom died, my dad and I moved to Cloudbury. You know. To start fresh."

"Is that why you're so obsessed with death magic?" Shy asked. "Why you want to bring back the dead?"

"What?" Vexx blinked. "No. No! You're reading too much into that."

Shy and Kaylin exchanged skeptical glances, which annoyed Vexx even further.

"If anything, that would mean I'd try to learn healing magic," Vexx pointed out with a grimace. "And I've never had the touch for that."

"If you say so, Master."

"So what's your story, succubus?" he asked after a few uncomfortable moments of silence.

"Oh, that is a long tale. Much too long to tell, with Cloudbury not far off. And with…somewhat innocent ears around."

Kaylin blushed, her long elven ears twitching, but she said nothing. Shyola smirked over at her. "And what of you, elf? What's your stor—"

"Goblins!" Kaylin shouted as she fumbled for her bow. "On the left," she added, then swore as she dropped her nocked arrow, quickly crouching to snatch it from the road. A grove of trees near the road rustled, and then one goblin darted out, followed by another and another.

Vexx readied his flames and aimed at the first goblin, a stocky brute who stomped forward with an upraised spear —and then Vexx shifted upward, firing three fireballs at the trees. The trees shook even as the branches caught fire, a goblin lookout concealed on one limb came crashing to the ground. A few others staggered out of the grove, grunting and barking as they slapped uselessly at their smoking pelts.

Kaylin had recovered now, and she loosed a quick shot that took the goblin in its leg, just as three others rushed past. Then, Shy stepped forward, her glowing whip flickering into existence, and she slashed forward at all three. They toppled forward, severed through, and collapsed to the ground.

"Silly goblins," Shy added with a laugh. A few others had come to a ragged halt, and as one, they turned and ran off up the nearest hill. Kaylin held her bow at full draw for a long moment and then lowered it, easing off the pressure. Vexx dispelled his magic. His hands fell to his sides and he took a long breath.

"I hope you didn't intend for one of those filthy creatures to be a meal," Shy said, striding back to the road. "A goblin simply won't do."

"No," Vexx said, glancing down the road. "I had another idea."

28

BREAKFAST

"This is a joke, I take it," Shyola said after a long moment. The dungeoneers were standing in Pollander's ranch, just outside Cloudbury. Shyola's unimpressed gaze rested on a large sheep as it cropped the grass inside its pasture. Kaylin crouched beside the sheep, feeling its soft wool.

"It's no joke," Vexx replied. "Goblins have been raiding the ranch here. The owner is busy at the tavern. Nobody's around to notice," Vexx said, spreading his hands wide, gesturing at the tranquil pasture in the hills outside Cloudbury. "I don't know if it's a virgin or not, but otherwise, it's perfect! Go on, dig in."

Kaylin giggled as the sheep sniffed at her fingers. "Oh, she's so cute and fluffy."

Shyola regarded it with intense distaste. "I can't believe this is what you had in mind, Master."

"Why not? Plenty of people like sheep. Goblins like sheep. I like sheep." Vexx shrugged. "I'm sure it'll struggle. What's the problem?"

"The problem is, is that it's such a mediocre sacrifice.

Centuries I was trapped in there. To say I was looking forward to feasting on a virgin would be an immense understatement." Shy leaned in close, gesturing at Kaylin, who was laughing as she played with the sheep. "I mean, she'd be *acceptable*, I guess. And after I sampled her hair, I kind of want the whole meal. Does she even have any family?" she whispered. "Little elf girls like that go missing all the time. No one will—"

"Shy. Enough."

She sighed before cracking her knuckles and sashaying towards the sheep. "Out of the way, girl," she said, pushing a protesting Kaylin to the side. Then, there was a blur of motion, Vexx raising a hand in front of his face, Kaylin reeling aside as fur and blood went flying. There was a tearing, rending, lustful sound, as if a gathering of starving orc barbarians were having an eating contest.

Finally, a silence settled.

Then, there was a long belch. "Sorry," Shy said, looking back at them, trying unsuccessfully to wipe blood from her chin, but dribbling it all over her half-exposed breasts instead. "I was famished. Not bad, all things considered, but I still have a hunger…" Shy finished, locking her gaze with Kaylin.

Kaylin just shook her head. "That poor sheep," she said sadly.

Shy nodded in agreement. "It should have been you."

Vexx clapped his hands. "Well, it's great to see you two are getting along! Now that you won't be at each other's throats, how about we head into town? We need to get ourselves another quest, and I'd rather not have anyone see us near…" he prodded the ripped-apart sheep carcass with a boot. "This."

Kaylin made a face at the carcass. "You're such a messy eater. Who raised you?"

"Don't start this with me, girl!" Shy threatened, snapping her whip into existence, grinning triumphantly when Kaylin yelped and leapt away. "Centuries ago, people had some respect for their eld—"

"Enough of that!" Vexx snapped. "Calm down, Shy. Let's just get going."

Shy sighed, her whip dematerializing. "You're right, Master. I don't want to get all worked up like that right after eating," she added, patting her toned stomach. "I'm eager to see how civilization has developed in my absence."

29

DOCTOR FANSEE'S QUEST

"This town looks just like any other one," Shyola grumbled once they'd entered Cloudbury. "There are some fancier crossbows, and some of the buildings look different, but it wouldn't be out of place centuries ago. Though…I remember most of the towns being on fire."

"Really," Vexx said, half-listening as he led the way through the market. "Was that before or after you got there?"

Shy chuckled, a seductive sound that was somehow ominous and flirtatious at the same time. "Stick with me for a while, Master, and I will tell you a few tales."

Vexx grunted, spotting Doctor Fansee's sign, and stepped up to the stall. This time, the potions vendor was frowning down at a few shriveled lizards. "Just won't do," he muttered to himself. "This won't…" he glanced up, then broke into a wide smile. "Customers! What brings you to Doctor Fansee's Pick-Me-Ups?" the gnome asked, then grinned as he took in Kaylin and Shyola. "Well, hello there! Goodness me, I'd be worried if I didn't have health potions around, with a couple of heart stoppers like you two!"

"Yeah, yeah," Vexx said, moving in closer as Kaylin blushed and Shyola twirled a finger around a lock of hair. "We need potions, same deal as before."

"Ah. Hey, kid."

"What, you don't recognize me?"

The gnome shrugged. "Ah, you humans all look the… oh, hey! The 'fighting one goblin' kid! How's you doing there, slugger?"

"I did just fine."

The gnome chuckled. "I'm guessing that goblin didn't do so well."

"Enough about the goblin. Gimme some more of those," Vexx said, tapping on a few of the blue potions and picking up a health potion or two. Kaylin also picked up a couple health potions for herself, but Shy seemed disinterested with the whole business.

"Hey, uh…you're dungeoneers, aren't you?" Doctor Fansee asked after a moment. "Doing odd jobs, that sort of thing?"

"Absolutely," Vexx and Kaylin said together.

"What's a dungeoneer?" Shy asked, as she examined a jar containing a preserved snake. Doctor Fansee fixed Vexx with an earnest gaze.

"Here's the thing. I can't afford to post a bounty right now…I'm in a bit of, well, I guess you could call it financial distress." He grimaced. "Look, I'm flat out broke."

"Really? You seem to be doing well to me."

"Appearances can be deceiving. Speaking of which, I have an illusion potion here for twenty silvers. But I'll get right down to it, young man. I get my herbs in an area that I'm not quite comfortable disclosing to half the town.

But a pack of wargs have moved in. You know, I tried waiting them out. Figured they'd just leave after a while. But it's been days now! Just yesterday, I tried luring them away with meat—just about lost my hand for the trouble! Anyway…I want them gone."

"Wargs?" Vexx grimaced. "Oof. How many are we talking about?"

"Heheh, never mind how many, kiddo. Anyway, I can give you some of my potions—after I've made them. But right now, this is all I have," Doctor Fansee said, gesturing at his array of potions. It was an impressive amount, but now that Vexx looked, he could see that there were a lot of gaps where potions hadn't been refilled.

Vexx hesitated. *I don't like the idea of tussling with wargs, not one bit.* He looked over at Kaylin, who shared his concerned expression. *Beasts like that are on a whole different level. Goblins we can handle, but—*

"We'll do it," Shy declared.

"Shy!"

"What? I've been trapped for ages, let a girl have her fun. I'm ready to spill some blood," she said, grinning at Vexx. "And to f—"

"First things first," Doctor Fansee broke in. "I'll close up shop and take you there myself. I'm not drawing maps for you to go giving out to all your friends."

"I wouldn't do that," Vexx protested.

"Yeah, we don't have any friends!" Kaylin added cheerfully.

"Good," Doctor Fansee said, already stuffing potions in a crate beside his stall. "Give me a minute to get ready, and we'll be off. It won't take me long to get what I need once the coast is clear."

The dungeoneers waited as Doctor Fansee closed up

his shop. Shyola seemed calm enough, watching as people went about their day and occasionally licking her lips, but Kaylin clearly shared some of Vexx's concerns.

He sidled up next to her. "So, wargs. What do you think?"

"I've never fought a warg before," she confessed. "But I've heard stories about them from the wood elves and a few of the elders in the village. Huge, wolf-like creatures that can rip an elk apart in seconds."

"Well…just make your shots count. With your arrows and my fireballs, we can take them down from a distance. And Shy can take out any who get close. You might not like her, but it's clear she can handle herself."

Kaylin nodded uncertainly, and they waited together until Doctor Fansee approached, a heavy pack resting on his shoulders. He smiled up at them, as if eager to be on this adventure.

"So whaddaya say, buddy? You ready?"

"The name's Vexx White. And I say…" Vexx extended his hand and clasped it around the gnome's little hand. "I say you have yourself a deal."

30

ALONG THE STREAM

"Here's good," the potion vendor said, now that they had gotten a bit out of town, setting his pack down and rummaging through it, glass vials clinking together. He held up a yellow potion and turned to face the dungeoneers.

"Good for what?" Vexx asked.

"Look, I don't want you being able to retrace the route," Doctor Fansee said. "That's why I want you all to take a sip of this Confusion potion. It won't last long, trust me."

"Getting drugged by a stranger?" Kaylin frowned. "I don't know, seems like a bad idea."

"For once, I agree with the elf," Shy broke in. "I'm not drinking your brew. Blindfold me if you want, gnome, gag me, even. I don't mind. But no potions."

"Well…I suppose blindfolds will do."

Vexx shrugged. "Works for me."

"Good, good," Doctor Fansee said, before rummaging around in his pack. "Let's see, what can I use…"

A wagon rumbled down the road, a caravan leaving

Cloudbury by the same gate, three fully laden horse-wagons with a half dozen guards marching on either side. Atop the first wagon was seated a stoic dwarf with a gleaming helm and a crossbow, who looked over as they made their way past. Vexx raised a hand in salutation, but the dwarf ignored him.

He lowered his hand and coughed as the wagons rolled past, kicking up a flurry of dust, and turned to see Doctor Fansee looking up at him.

"Crouch down here, lad, and I'll tie it up," he said. Before too long, the dungeoneers were blindfolded, Vexx tilting his head to make out what was happening.

"Just hold on to my pack, lass," the gnome said, Shy grunting something in reply. "The rest of you hold hands. Up there. No…here, let me help you."

Vexx felt his arms push, and then felt warmth as he clenched Kaylin's and Shyola's hands.

"Step lightly now," Doctor Fansee said, and Vexx followed as Shy pulled him forward, Kaylin trailing behind. They shambled along together, Kaylin squeezing tightly, and despite himself, Vexx found himself smiling. It didn't last long, fading away as he scraped a low-hanging branch and cursed. The gnome cackled up ahead. "It won't be too much farther!"

VEXX DIDN'T ENTIRELY KNOW what "too much farther" meant to gnomes, but it clearly wasn't what it meant to humans. *They're shorter too—you'd think it wouldn't be far at all. Why does he keep dragging us through this forest?* Behind him, Kaylin stumbled, pulling hard on Vexx's arm. It was a sensation he was getting more and more used to.

"Hold on," he grunted, pausing and hauling Kaylin back up. "Doctor, are we there yet? This is getting ridiculous."

"Ah, no, not quite," the gnome began, but fell silent when the dungeoneers followed with a chorus of groans and complaints. "Oh, fine! We're close enough, I suppose. You can take your blindfolds off."

Vexx released his hands, tearing his blindfold off and blinking at the afternoon light. He'd been hearing the faint trickle of water for some time and now caught a glimpse of the winding stream through the forest they were sheltered in. Beside him, Kaylin took a few steps forward to peer past the nearby trees, her eyes sparkling with curiosity.

"You harvest the herbs along the stream bank?" she asked.

"I do indeed," Doctor Fansee proclaimed with a smile. "Oh, it's only a little creek, fed from the rainfall in the Lifeless Hills, but it provides the perfect growing conditions for some rather useful herbs. You won't find it on any map," he added, tapping his head. "But I know where to find it!"

"I see your problem," Kaylin said quietly, and Vexx pushed forward to get a better view. After a moment, he saw a few dark brown shapes moving along the near bank. At first, they looked like cows; massive creatures stalked the area, but Vexx quickly made out their wolf-like features.

"Yes," Doctor Fansee replied. "You can see them from here. You know, one interesting thing about wargs is that their eyesight isn't that good. No, they hunt mostly by scent."

"By scent?" Vexx asked.

"Oh yes, they can track prey hundreds of yards away, and once the scent is on, there's no escape. No, that's why I was thinking we should take especially good care to approach from downwind. Otherwise, we'll be in quite a lot of danger!"

Wordlessly, Kaylin bent down and plucked up a clump of dried grass, tossing it in the air. It drifted directly toward the wargs by the river bank.

"Oh dear."

The head of one of the wargs shot up, and he sniffed the air, just as another and another looked over.

31

WARG SLAYING

"Oh, fuck!" Doctor Fansee cursed as the wargs began bounding towards them. "Well, best of luck!" he added, scampering away into the underbrush.

"Damn it all!" Vexx cursed, glancing left and right, then waved for Shyola and Kaylin to join him. "We'll hold in this clearing here! Backs against these trees!"

"I'm with you, Master," Shyola replied calmly as they moved into position. We're in a meadow here, which means we can get some quick shots off even if they dart through. Unless they circle behind us…I don't even want to think about that.

Vexx's thoughts faltered as he saw Kaylin tarrying, fumbling with something as she pulled a tree limb down. "Kaylin, what are you doing?" She wound a rope around the tree limb, tossing the net to the ground.

"Don't worry about her, Master," Shyola advised. "The wargs will devour her first and we can take them as they're feeding."

"Just one second!" Kaylin called back, binding rope to a second tensed branch and gingerly stepping back. Then she whirled around, sprinting towards them, her bow catching on stray leaves and branches.

"Get ready to shoot!" Vexx hissed. "Just as soon as they clear that brush."

He stood there, magical energies drifting from both readied fists, listening to the snapping and crashing of the wargs hurtling through the forest. To his left, Shyola materialized her whip, and Kaylin nocked an arrow to his right. A roar echoed in the distance, followed by another and another, and the first warg burst into the clearing. Kaylin loosed her arrow, Vexx fired an accompanying fireball, yet somehow, the warg dodged both of their attacks.

It landed on the ground, head raised as if in contempt, and took one step forward. That step snagged just where Kaylin had placed her trap. In an instant, the coiled tree limbs sprang out, whipping the howling warg up into the air and trapping him in a rope net.

"Yes!" Kaylin cried out.

"That's just the first," Vexx replied. "Get ready for—"

He fell silent as another three emerged, bounding towards them. An arrow shot forward, embedding itself in a massive warg's shoulder, but it didn't even slow. The claws of the wargs tore great gashes in the meadow below as they charged forward, one taking a fireball right in the face but just shrugging it off.

Vexx saw a blur of motion as he fired fireball after fireball—Shyola rushing forward. A beam of crackling crimson energy shot out as Shyola charged the warg in the center. She raised her hand up—just as the warg howled and lowered its head. Shy leaped over, scrambling up the fur, then gripped the warg tightly by the scruff of its neck.

"You are mine!"

Her eyes glowed, the warg howled in confusion and

rage as its eyes glowed crimson, and then it raised itself. Shy pulled it to the right, where the warg barrelled into the shoulder of another. She materialized her whip, slashing it forward to curl around the neck of the second warg, and then ripped it aside—the magical whip cutting clear through the warg's head and severing it entirely.

The third warg had been shrugging off Vexx's frantic fireballs like they were nothing. Vexx was backing away, no, abandoning his dignity, as he scrambled behind a tree. A quickly fired arrow sunk into the huge warg's side, but did little to slow the giant creature. Vexx spared only a single glimpse at Shyola's mastery of her warg before fixing his vision on the slavering jaws of the warg barreling towards him.

It's so fast and strong! I wasn't ready, I—I'm not ready to die!

The warg paused in confusion and turned its head to sniff warily as Shyola and her warg approached. Then there was a blur of motion as she slashed down where the warg had been a moment before. The warg had turned around now, slashing at the possessed warg, who let out an unearthly howl as a great tear was ripped into its flank. Vexx popped out, blasting fireballs at the warg, doing little other than singing its fur.

Shyola's warg was dying now, but she leaped off just in time, whirling in the air and hooking her magical whip around one of the warg's hind legs. She pulled away, the leg cutting in half and sending the warg to the ground. Arrows and fireballs pelted the ground where the wounded warg lay, slamming into its hide, and after a few agonizing seconds, it finally stopped moving.

Vexx staggered forward a few moments later, clearing

away the rank smell of singed fur and flesh. "They're so tough," he muttered.

Shy, meanwhile, was stretching idly beside the three dead wargs. "Leave these creatures to me, Master. You're not quite at their level."

"I see that…"

Kaylin brushed past, no worse for wear, pointing up at the fourth warg. It still struggled in the rope net, snarling as it tore at the coarse fabric. "Did you see that? It worked!"

32

TO FIGHT AND KILL

"It's chewing on your rope, Kaylin. I don't think it wants to be a pet," Vexx said, eyeing the warg suspended above as it broke through another one of the ropes, the net unraveling at an alarming pace. He stepped back nervously, wondering how to kill it from down here, and glanced over at Shyola.

"Shy, can you do the honors?" Vexx asked, brushing sweat from his head. "Since you're so good with these."

She shot him a peculiar look and made no movement to help.

"Hurry," Vexx said, "before—"

Kaylin cried out as the warg toppled to the ground, almost crushing her. She stumbled aside, but then the warg lurched forward, pinning her to the ground.

"Shy!" Vexx shouted as he blasted the warg's side with a fireball.

She was smirking, still lounging in place. "Oh, I know I said that *I* wouldn't kill her. But the warg..." she shrugged. "Whatever happens, happens."

Vexx cursed as Kaylin screamed, struggling under the

weight of the warg, slashing upward with her knife and slicing away flesh and fur. Vexx sprinted over, readying a burst of flames, and just as the warg snarled and opened its massive jaws, Vexx raised his fist.

The rush of magical energy at point blank range burned through the warg, and it toppled to the ground, leaning partway on Kaylin. Vexx rushed over and hauled her out to stagger beside the burned warg. On the other side of the warg, Shy smirked as she ran a hand through her long hair.

"That one's all yours, Master. Nice work."

Vexx tried to snap back in irritation, but he did feel a strange surge of energy within him, as if he'd gained the ability to learn a new trick. So instead, he just brushed off a few sticky strings of warg saliva that had stuck to his robes.

"Good work, lad and lasses," Doctor Fansee said.

Vexx looked around in surprise and irritation. Somehow, in all the chaos, he'd forgotten that the gnome was still around. "You! You left us to fight and die!"

"Ah, well, to fight and kill," he said as he emerged from a thicket of bushes. He paused to pop a few wild berries in his mouth, closing his eyes in delight as he chewed away. "And you did quite well. Mmm, these are lovely. Now then! You've made good progress, but ah…" he strode over, then gestured towards the nearby stream. He pointed somewhere just past the meadow where the fighting had happened, on a forested ridge that overlooked the water, and the dungeoneers came in close. "You see those?"

Vexx felt his spirits sink, but he kept his voice light and unbothered. "Four more wargs."

"That's right. The rest of the pack. But, hey, you're

halfway done!" The gnome smiled, spreading his arms wide as he took in Shyola—looking indifferent, arms clasped under her ample bosom, Kaylin—wearing a skeptical expression as she counted her arrows, and Vexx—peering over at the wargs resting beside the stream. Doctor Fansee grinned and clapped his hands together. "The herbs are just over there. Come on, come on!"

"Give me a moment," Vexx said as he approached the nearest fallen warg. He knelt down and placed a hand on its hide before closing his eyes to concentrate on his energies. Vexx forced the necromantic magic into the warg's corpse. Moments passed. And still…nothing.

"What's going on?" he said, finally, frowning down at the body.

Shyola nodded to herself. "Ah, have you tried with creatures like these before? No, of course not. You likely are too far from the same level of power to be able to control it."

"Level?"

"Yes. You'll notice if you feel a surge of energy. That's when you can learn new tricks or boost your powers."

"Oh…oh!" Vexx blinked, excitedly rising to his feet. "I just felt that after this fight."

"Aww," Shyola cooed. "To be young again. Back when gaining an ability was such an easy thing that a little squabble like this would be enough to boost your power. I'd have to damn whole cities just to feel that kind of a rush."

Vexx snorted. "We'll wait on it for now. Let's just get this over with." He left the warg behind, acutely discouraged that he couldn't raise it to help with the rest of his pack. Somehow, even after being at this new 'level' of power, he didn't think he could do it. But those were thoughts for a less pressing time.

"That was a nice trap you used," the gnome said approvingly to Kaylin. "Good thinking, elf! I've been thinking, dungeoneers," he added, looking at all of them. "I can help out a bit on this next fight. You see, if I attract their attention, I can have them follow this game trail here…"

33

AMBUSHING THE WARGS

Vexx stretched his legs, growing increasingly cramped in his concealed position behind a weeping willow and looked over at the other dungeoneers. They were hard to find as well, all crouched behind rocks and bushes that overlooked the game trail. *I just hope they really do come up this way.* Over the light wind, he heard the soft padding of Doctor Fansee, his hurried footsteps moving quickly over the dirt trail.

"Follow me, you overgrown mutts! I'm so tasty!"

He hurtled over a small bush, his little legs pumping away, kicking stray dirt and rocks behind him as he ran his way up the game trail. *It's a clear shot from here, at least.* Vexx watched Doctor Fansee come closer, a perfect target, and the wargs undoubtedly close behind him. The gnome hurried past and tossed a vial on the path behind him. Vexx fixed his attention on the potion inside. *Just hit it with a fireball, the gnome had said.* Vexx snapped his finger, a spark of flame blossoming, and he aimed directly at the potion. But still, they waited.

A snarl was the first thing that announced their

approach, and then a huge muzzle worked its way through the brush, sniffing away. Vexx tensed. They were supposed to be cautious. If they realized they were running into an ambush position…

The moment lingered, but then the warg howled as it bounded up the game trail to where the dungeoneers laid in wait.

Good, Vexx thought, seeing another warg appear. *If we have to fight, then it should be on ground of our own choosing.*

An arrow sailed past, clipping a rope, and then several huge weighted nets dropped to the ground as the wargs ran up the slope. Several wargs yelped, startled, but others pushed their way past. Vexx heard the chuckle of the gnome in the distance.

"Hit it, boy!"

Vexx fired a powerful fireball straight at the glass vial, and an instant later, it erupted with a spectacular explosion, dousing the trapped wargs around them in a greenish haze. The gnome cackled as the procession of wargs now stumbled about in a confused, obstructed mess.

"That poison will do them good! Now, don't waste this moment, dungeoneers!"

Vexx grunted, standing up high, both hands sending fireball after fireball that knocked the struggling wargs off their feet just as they managed to rise. Kaylin rose from the forest, looking every bit an elf as she narrowed her eyes and released an arrow that caught a warg in the throat. Shyola stepped forward casually before lunging forward and unfurling her whip to its maximum distance, catching a warg with a solid crack but keeping away from the poisonous mist.

Doctor Fansee rushed forward and danced maniacally

by the commotion. Vexx tried to ignore the bizarre sight, instead pounding the wargs with fireball after fireball, until finally he felt woozy and reached for a magic potion. He popped it open, swigging deeply, then fired at one warg that had managed to free itself from the net.

The great beast rocked to the side, breathing heavily as it suffered from the poisonous gasses, then Kaylin's arrow took it through the heart. Doctor Fansee did a backflip at the sight.

"Very good, very good!" he shouted. "Just a couple left!"

Vexx was moving forward now, out into the open, picking his targets one by one. The wargs were tough, but Vexx allowed himself a moment of consternation. Just one of his fireballs could take down a goblin and even a few around them, but...

Ugh, I have to hammer away at these wargs. The good doctor said he'd give me all the magic potions I need after this, though, so there's no point in holding back!

At that, Vexx fired two fireballs that knocked down another, reaching again for his half-filled magic potion. By the time he'd corked and put it down, the final warg was dead. Shyola stood over it triumphantly as she vanished her whip.

She breathed in for a long moment. "It smells like victory, Master."

"Ah, that could be the poison mist," the gnome suggested as he clambered to his feet. "Your 'master' did a good job of exploding that little vial."

"No, no, that's mostly faded away," the succubus replied, coughing and waving a hand in the air. "Though you young ones might want to keep away for another minute."

Kaylin emerged from the forest, barely glancing at the fallen wargs and Shyola. She turned to Vexx and her ears twitched in excitement. "Do you hear it?" she asked, smiling at Vexx.

"Hear...what?"

"The stream!"

Now that the silence had settled, Vexx could indeed make out the gentle babbling of the nearby stream. He cracked his knuckles and stretched. "Are you ready, Doctor?"

"Absolutely," the potion vendor replied as he stepped over the mangled corpses of the wargs. "Let's get those herbs!"

34

GATHERING HERBS

The hidden glade just outside Cloudbury seemed as if it was from another world entirely. With the dead wargs behind them, Vexx could almost pretend life was peaceful and carefree. The soft croaking of frogs broke the silence, along with Doctor Farnasee's cheerful whistling as he bustled about from one crop of herbs to the other.

"So you don't need us to do anything?" Vexx asked again, still feeling somewhat dubious. It seemed strange to suddenly be so unneeded.

"Not a thing, my boy, not a thing. Just take it easy for now. I'm going to get as much as I can carry. You never know what might move in here next time I need supplies. Centaurs, probably."

Kaylin splashed into the shallows, hands dipped into the water, and splashed them on her face. "It's nice and cool here, Vexx!" She poured a handful of water into her mouth.

Sluggishly, Vexx moved to join her. "You're sure looking cheerful," he said. "Those wargs were no joke though, huh?"

"Oh yes! It'll be quite the tale when I return to my forest village next."

"Oh? Are you looking to do that?"

"Hmm? Oh, not any time soon. You know, after that last battle, I felt something strange. Like...I'd gained a new ability somehow, but I don't know what! I got one of those feelings earlier, back when I learned how to use those nets."

"Oh yeah," Vexx said, blinking. "I did too."

Shyola's soft chuckle echoed around them. She bent to pick up a stone and flung it along the water's surface, sending it skipping two or three times along the stream. "Ah, to be young again! You see, you both need to choose a new skill. You've increased the level of your combat power...somehow."

Vexx nodded. "So we can learn new skills? That sure makes magic easier. It took years of study to get to this point."

"Easier?" Shyola shrugged. "You have to kill a good deal to get to that point, and by the time you get where I am...I can drain a room full of souls, but that barely makes a dent in my progress. But it is fun, so I'm not complaining at all."

"Hmm..." Kaylin said, grabbing a stone of her own. She tried to skip it across the placid surface of the stream but it simply sank at once. "I wonder what I'll go for. Any ideas, Vexx?"

"For you? I don't know, not being so damn clumsy. That would be good." He grinned as Kaylin stuck her tongue out at him. "I think, maybe...I need a stronger kind of fire magic. I wasn't doing much more than tickling those wargs."

"Another piece of advice, darling," Shyola called out,

now lounging against a tree. "Don't fight things much tougher than you are. I want you to live for a long while, Master. I have plans for you." She winked.

"Duly noted," Vexx muttered, but he was thinking of different ways he could improve his fireballs. "A scorching missile, maybe?" he said to himself, thinking of combining the longer-term effects of his burst of flames with his normal fireball attack.

"Why do you like fire so much?" Kaylin asked, poking her bow at a frog, which hopped away with a slightly frantic croak. "Why not frost or something?"

"Because fire is awesome," Vexx replied as he snapped his fingers and made an approving sound when the flames warmed his face. He blew it out, then settled down with a sigh. *A scorching missile, I think that's the way to go.* "Why do you like your bow so much?"

"Well, my family always said elves have to be good with a bow," Kaylin responded in a very serious tone. "And I've always been…less graceful than an elf should be. So I guess…I guess I didn't want to disappoint them in everything."

"Oh. So you don't really care about the bow?"

"No, it's not that," Kaylin replied as she clutched her bow to her chest. "I like it fine. It's just…it'd be so much easier if the arrow just went where I wanted it to go, you know?"

"Oh, like a guided missile? Couldn't you learn that skill? It's common enough with mages."

"Huh…" Kaylin blinked, looked down at her bow. "A guided missile…"

Vexx had already lost interest in the conversation, having decided to pursue a scorching missile of his own. He closed his eyes, focusing his training on his new ability, then snapped his eyes open. He focused on a nearby pine tree and pointed at it. With a rush of energy, he fired a monstrous fireball that hissed as it rushed by. Shy whistled appreciatively as it slammed into the tree and split into a few smaller fires that landed on the ground nearby and sizzled. The fireball had caught in the branches above and the crackling of the blackened wood grew louder until the fire spread to engulf the entire tree.

"You scared me there, sonny!" Doctor Fansee called out as he warily backed away from the tree, holding freshly cut herbs in one hand and a small knife in the other. "At least warn me!"

Vexx just grinned. "Well, I made my decision. What do you think, Kaylin?"

She clapped approvingly. "That will come in handy if we need to burn any trees. Hey Vexx, you got something you can throw?"

"Uh… yeah," he said, rummaging around in his robes and producing the empty bottle of magic potion. "Will this do?"

"Perfect," she said, already nocking an arrow and drawing her bow. "Throw it up real high!"

"Alright, here goes!" Vexx shouted, tossing it up in the air.

Kaylin loosed an arrow in an instant, and as Vexx watched, it went a bit wide…then suddenly curved toward it, the tip of the arrow flared a vibrant blue. The arrowhead took the empty glass through the middle and it cracked open, sprinkling shards of glass down. Doctor Fansee yelped, cursing the apprentice dungeoneers. Vexx looked over at Kaylin with a raised eyebrow.

Kaylin lowered her bow. "A guided missile, like you said!"

Shyola snorted. "A potion-seeking arrow? Yeah, like that's going to be useful. Ah, but it is peculiar to watch your excitement." She crossed one long leg over the other and idly examined her fingernails. "Young apprentice dungeoneers grow up so quickly. A job like a succubus is far too prestigious to learn new skills after playing around with a pack of overgrown mutts."

"How is succubus a job?" Kaylin asked. "Or prestigious?"

Shyola tore her eyes away from her nails to glower at the elf. Doctor Fansee grumbled to himself, knocking shards of glass out of his hair, then resumed harvesting herbs. Vexx walked over to the stream, found a nice spot on a boulder beside Kaylin, and stretched out with a yawn.

"Feels nice here, huh?" she asked, throwing a stone along the stream. "Oh hey, it bounced once!" Kaylin grinned over at Vexx, who was wedging himself into a comfortable position, trying his best to enjoy the tranquil setting and warm sunlight.

35

VISITORS TO CLOUDBURY

"Draining a fish's soul is quite unsatisfying," Shyola remarked as they strolled through the forest outside Cloudbury. "They don't experience pain in quite the same thrilling way."

"You didn't have to eat it," Kaylin grumbled. "It was Vexx and I who did all the fishing."

"What's that?" Shyola asked. "Do I hear my next meal talking? Vexx, can we put an end to this elf slowing us down? Her bleating is beginning to wear on me."

"No," he said, making his way past a copse of trees. *There's a logging road nearby—there has to be. Damn that gnome for insisting we take a different route back to Cloudbury. Who cares where his stupid herbs are?*

"Do you hear that?" Kaylin broke in, her elven ears twitched as she bounded forward. "Come on!" she said urgently, whirling around and waving them forward. "I think there's a fight up ahead!"

"A fight?" Vexx asked. "Shouldn't we be avoiding those?"

"Come on, darling," Shyola said as she gripped his arm

and excitedly dragged him along. Her eyes swirled with glee as she pushed forward. "There could be souls for the reaping!"

"Alright, alright," Vexx said, shrugging her off and joining the other dungeoneers as they rushed forward. They passed bush after bush and dodged under low-hanging branches, the commotion sending frantic birds into flight as they crashed through the brush. After a few moments, Vexx heard the sounds of battle. The familiar grunting of goblins, a soft twang of a crossbow, and shouts of a struggle. A feminine voice cried out in pain, then was abruptly cut off, the wail reducing to a faint gurgle as they drew closer.

Vexx saw it now, a wagon tilted off the road, a half-circle of desperate figures fending off a swarm of goblins. And not doing too well, judging from the fallen bodies on the road. Kaylin came to an abrupt halt and crouched by the edge of the forest. Vexx stormed forward, launching fireball after fireball, and a charging wave of goblins stumbled to the ground as the dungeoneers caught them from behind. One goblin stumbled past, but a man in tattered robes cracked a heavy crossbow over its head.

The rest of the goblins turned in surprise, a cluster of three spear-armed goblins slashed in half as Shyola swung her magical whip through them. She lunged forward to grab a fourth by the head, and it squealed in fright as she grinned. There was a swirl of energy around them, a spreading crimson wave as she drained the goblin's soul, the whirlwind obscuring them as she cackled darkly.

That was enough to drive the other hesitating goblins away. They dashed off in all directions, one stumbling to the ground with Kaylin's arrow jutting out from its neck, a few others falling to the ground, burning and screaming.

But Vexx didn't push it, pausing when he felt his stamina reserves depleted, simply standing by to watch as several other goblins fled through the forest. Instead, he strode forward, glancing at the mess the smirking succubus had made of her feast, and then nodding at the heavily breathing man in robes as he tossed his smashed crossbow to the ground. He seemed to be the only survivor.

"Vexx White, dungeoneer for hire," Vexx announced. "Seems like you had a bit of a problem along the road."

The man spat, a pinkish mix of blood and spittle, and wiped his nose where a goblin must have broken it. "I'll say. They told me the Lifeless Hills was a rough country, but..." he spread his arms wide, taking in his fallen companions. He shook his head in despair.

"Did you take any guards?"

He sighed. "You're standing on one of them."

Vexx glanced down, shuffling to the side. "Ah, sorry," he said, examining his bloodstained boot. The fallen caravan guard seemed to have been split almost in half.

"My name is Sophokleus Vaiglar," the caravan leader said sadly. "Renowned fashion designer. Perhaps you've heard of me."

"I'm afraid not."

Sophokleus sighed. "Fashion is such a fickle business. One moment you're winning an award for magical pauldron of the year, the next, your partner and models are lying dead in the road in the middle of nowhere. So much for the fashion week."

"Tragic," Vexx said, taking in the scene. The wagon seemed an utter wreck, bundles of clothing spilled out around it, but aside from the fallen goblins, there didn't seem to be any other treasure. Shyola and Kaylin were already going over the corpses, apparently content to let

Vexx do the chatting. He peered over into the fallen wagon.

"What's that you've got there?" he asked, spotting a huge chest laying on its side, crammed in with all sorts of clothing.

"Eh?" Sophokleus had bent down, trying to wipe blood off a pile of tunics. He glanced over and frowned. "Ah, that was Naruan's lockbox. I guess there's no getting into it now. He was a mage, you know, and a talented designer and model. Have you heard of enchanted codpieces? He came up with that, you know, though he didn't have the sense to file for a patent. Now there are all sorts of knockoffs, and half of them just end up—"

"Hey, so this isn't yours?" Vexx asked, nodding at the chest. Shyola and Kaylin were approaching now, the succubus turning a goblin axe around in her hand, examining it for defects.

"Oh, it is," Sophokleus protested. "It's just that it's locked, and Naruan wasn't exactly the key type. I don't suppose any of you can pick it?"

"I know one dwarf," Kaylin suggested, but Vexx shook his head.

The caravan master shook his head in distress. "Ah, it's an ensorcelled chest, after all. There's a code to open it, but he was the only one who knew it…" he pointed his finger in disgust at another fallen traveller, his robes still gleaming as it thrummed with the power of a magical enchantment.

"Is that so…Kaylin, could you help him with the rest?" Vexx asked, his gaze focused on the fallen mage.

"Hmm? Sure thing, Vexx. So what did you need a hand with?"

Vexx waited for the two to move around to the other side of the fallen wagon before taking a few quick strides to the corpse of the fallen mage. He knelt next to the mage, a dark-skinned middle-aged traveller with a jagged gash in his chest. Vexx held one open palm above the man's head and fed it energy. A moment later, the man's eyes popped open, radiating a peculiar green, and he rumbled something.

"Hush," Vexx said. "I have a question for you. The chest. What is the code to open it?"

The man stirred, as if trying to rise to his feet, and Vexx put a hand on the corpse's bloody chest to restrain the undead magician. "The code."

"It's…" the man rasped. "Four…seven…eight…zero…two."

Vexx nodded to himself. "Alright, got it."

"Gob…lins…" the mage said. "Sudden…attack…"

"Yeah, I know," Vexx said, casually severing the link, and the corpse slumped back to the ground. He stood, brushed dirt off his knees, and walked over to the huge chest. It was an ornate design with strange markings all along the edge, and he felt the sensation of energy as he rested a gloved hand on its surface.

"That's about everything," the caravan master was saying, the wooden planks creaking as he stepped back into the wagon, an overloaded pack on his back. Sophokleus looked over at Vexx. "What are you doing?"

"If I can open this, can I take half of what's inside?" Vexx asked.

The man shrugged. "Well, I can't get it open. Sure, you can take half. I'd rather have half of something than all of nothing."

Vexx pressed his ear to the chest, nodding to himself as

he tapped against the wood with one hand, the second hand discreetly selecting the numbered symbols.

"Ah, the chest is speaking to me," he said, rapping away as he moved from one number to another. "It calls to a worthy mage. It wants to reveal itself to one of noble heart. It whispers, you see, it says..." he trailed off, selecting the last number, and stood up to look at the latch.

"What does it say?" Sophokleus asked in an awed whisper.

"That I am worthy," Vexx whispered, unlocking the latch and lifting up the ornate chest.

"Ooooh," Kaylin said, crowding in close. "How'd you do that?"

"A magician never reveals his secrets," Vexx said, grinning as he took in the gleaming silver teapot set. "Your friend, I see he liked his tea."

"Wouldn't shut up about it," Sophokleus agreed, craning his neck to get a better look. "What else is in there?"

Vexx carefully pushed the tea set to the side and brightened when he saw a few scrolls. He chose one at random and unrolled it, letting out a low whistle as he took in its contents.

"Erotic dryad art," Vexx said, shuffling through the rest of the scrolls. "This is quite the collection." He paused, adjusting one scroll. "That doesn't seem physically possible..."

"It is," Shyola said brightly. "One of these days, I'll show—"

"I'll take the tea set," the caravan master said. "You can take the scrolls."

"Oh, that's easy for you to say," Vexx grunted. "Silver is an easy sell. But these? I'm not sure where I'd start."

"What? They don't weigh a thing, and it's a good value. I tell you what," Sophokleus said after a moment. "There's something I need, now that...they're all dead." He paused, looking over Kaylin, Shyola, and Vexx—then nodded resolutely. "Yes, you three will do nicely. You said you're for hire, yes?"

Vexx raised an eyebrow. "What do you have in mind?"

36

CLOUDBURY FASHION WEEK

"It's Cloudbury Fashion Week, if you didn't know, and I'm running late."

"I don't keep up to date with community events," Vexx muttered. "Besides, I've been out of town for a while. Why do you need me for this, anyway?"

"Well, it's not like Naruan is up for it any more," Sophokleus snapped, pointing at the fallen mage. "He doesn't seem likely to leap up and model for me."

Vexx paused a moment, considering. "Ah…no. No, I suppose not."

"So it'll have to be you! I can't do it; I'll be too busy selling my merchandise. And these two fair young maidens will be showing off women's clothing."

"Never fear," Shyola purred. "I'm built for it," she said, shifting her hips below her flowing green robes. "Unlike this stick-thin elf."

"Hah!" Kaylin glared from below her huge teal hat. "You're as far from a fair young maiden as it's possible to get. Vexx?" She pouted her lips and smoothed a hand over her shimmering evening gown before batting her eyes at him. "Which one of us do you prefer?"

"Ah…"

"You're both wonderful," Sophokleus butted in. "Now, there's no time like the present! Cloudbury is up ahead, just show your stuff! We'll be the talk of the town! You know…I'm kind of glad they died," he said, gesturing over at the two corpses in sparkling robes. "They never had the same spark that you two have."

"Glad to hear it, darling," Shyola replied, starting down the road to Cloudbury. Kaylin hurried over in a huff.

Vexx raised an eyebrow at the fashion designer. "They're dead, and you move on so soon? You're quite the loyal one."

Sophokleus shrugged. "This is fashion, young man. There is no more cut-throat or ruthless industry in existence. It's nothing as carefree and happy-go-lucky as dungeoneering."

"I suppose not," Vexx muttered, falling into line behind Kaylin and Shyola, distracted by their low-cut clothing. *I've certainly done worse jobs than this.*

"Now work that robe!" Sophokleus said, clapping his hands as they rounded the corner and approached Cloudbury's gate. "Work it, Vexx, work it! You're a sexy magician, Vexx, a noble sorcerer from a far-off land! Shyola, you're perfect, Kaylin, you're a natural. Vexx! Put some sex in your step! Sell it for me, Vexx, sell it for me!"

37

A GOOD NIGHT'S SLEEP

Vexx wiped the sweat from his brow. *Who knew modeling was such grueling work? Not to mention demeaning.*

"You were wonderful, my lovelies," Sophokleussaid as he approached, the silver tea set rattling in its chest. "Shyola? Superb, superb, I've never sold so much in Cloudbury. Kaylin? Wonderful, absolutely wonderful! They loved the natural elf beauty look. I've made quite the killing today!"

"That's great!" Kaylin said with a smile. "Hey, which one of us did better? Me or Shy here?"

The fashion designer chuckled, then turned to Vexx. "Vexx, that was a…workmanlike performance. You really showed the people of Cloudbury that clothing can be worn."

"Great," Vexx muttered. "Just trying my best." *I can't believe I agreed to this. Dred Wyrm wouldn't have sunk this low.*

"Really? Your best?" Sophokleus blinked, then shook his head. "Well, either way, here our paths must part. I have a large quantity of dyed sheep's wool in Oerchenbrach that I'll need to pick up—I have a hunch it'll be in high demand soon enough."

Sophokleus left them, bustling about and picking up stray clothing while the dungeoneers exchanged glances. It had been a long day of modelling for the good people of Cloudbury, and they all seemed a bit tired. Kaylin sighed.

"Where to next, Vexx?"

"Well…" Vexx drummed the ornate chest that bore Naruan's silver tea set. "Where do you think we can sell a tea set?" Vexx asked. "A blacksmith, maybe?"

Shyola shrugged. "I've been away from human commerce for a few centuries. Do you still trade around bits of metal to buy souls?"

"They do," Kaylin said. "Shinier ones are better. Vexx told me that. Anyway, what if we went to the inn along the Western Gate? You know, where all the caravans come through? They probably serve a lot of strange people, and it seems like strange people seem to like tea."

Vexx raised an eyebrow. "That's a…surprisingly good idea. Well, it can't hurt. The day's almost over and we could afford a night at an inn. Let's check it out!"

"Oh yes," Shyola said. "We can sleep together for warmth, Master."

"Hey!" Kaylin glared. "I'm not sharing a bed with you, you big, old she-demon."

"Ohhh," the succubus purred, "I didn't mean I'd share it with you, you stupid little elf girl."

"Let's just see what they have," Vexx muttered and cursed as he hefted the heavy chest. The fading sun provided just enough light as they hurried through the streets, the crowds from earlier having dispersed long ago. A wagon trundled along, and based on the appearance of the caravan driver and her assistant, Vexx figured they were also visitors for Cloudbury's fashion week. Apparently this sleepy little town did a surprisingly decent amount of business once a year. Vex had never been openly ogled so much in his life.

He felt a sudden chill and clutched his robes closer around him. He picked up his pace, glancing back to see if Shy and Kaylin were still behind him. Another party of mounted adventurers clopped their way past, and then they were close to the Western Gate, the departure point for a number of caravans. Vexx paused for a moment, taking in the ramshackle huts and rickety houses near the gate.

"Over there," he said, pointing over to a multi-storied building with an aged gargoyle pagoda at the top. There were stables beside it and to the side stood what appeared to be an unused shed, though there didn't seem to be much in the way of customers. Vexx approached the ancient stone steps and slowly forced open a green-painted door, the hinges protesting at the motion. "Um, hello there? We're travellers."

"Ah, come in, come in!"

Vexx squinted in the dim lantern light. This was by far the most squalid of places he'd ever had the misfortune to visit, and it seemed to skimp on the lighting. He squeezed his way in, chest in hand, and waited for Shy and Kaylin to crowd in behind him. A woman stood at the other side of an old, gilded desk, smiling as she straightened up and waved them over.

"Three of you? For one night?"

"Not together!" Kaylin snapped.

The clerk smiled. "Certainly. Three rooms."

Shyola clapped Vexx on the back. "Two rooms will be—"

"Yes, three rooms," Vexx cut in. "Also, we were wondering if you would be interested in purchasing a silver tea set?"

The clerk chuckled politely. "Sir, I couldn't possibly answer that. The mistress of the house will be in this morning, and I can relay your request to her if you'd like. Three rooms then; we have the space. Shall I show you to your rooms?"

"Yes," Vexx said, as the clerk carefully selected three bronze keys. "How much will this be?"

"Five coppers," she said, and he tossed three in, prompting Kaylin to add two of her own.

Shyola patted her skimpy, skin-tight garments. "I have nothing to hide, as you see, and I've given the coins I plucked off those dead goblins to Vexx here. Everything I have is yours, Master..." she added, her hot breath tickling Vexx's ear.

The clerk raised an eyebrow but said nothing. "Just up these stairs," she said, leading them up the ancient, creaking staircase.

"I better get a good night's sleep," Kaylin grumbled as she walked. "I could have gotten a dozen arrows for two coppers."

"Oh, I think you'll be very impressed with our amenities," the clerk said with a well-rehearsed, mechanical politeness. "One room in here," she said, as she tapped a finger on the door. "One just across the hallway," she added, pointing at another. "And the last in the corner here. Any questions?"

"No, this will be fine," Vexx said, peering into one bland room. "Hey, is there any chance we can work off our room and board tomorrow?"

The clerk continued to keep her smile plastered on. "I

can relay your request to the mistress of the house in the morning, sir. She sometimes has odd jobs that guests can perform."

"Thank you," Vexx said, then rummaged in his pockets for an extra copper, which he dropped in the clerk's extended hand. "That's for all the trouble—and I hope you're extra convincing in the morning. With the mistress of the house."

"Yes, sir," she said, bowing and pocketing the coin. "I'll see what I can do. Rest well, sir. We get a lot of traffic outside in the morning, and with Cloudbury Fashion Week, the mistress of the house expects more guests than usual."

Vexx sighed . "I don't even want to think about Cloudbury Fashion Week…"

38

THE DAMNED SOULS

Dawn's rays peeked through the slats of the old inn's rickety walls as Vexx White made his way downstairs. The steps creaked under his feet as he strode past, the tea set in its chest resting in the crook of his arm. He yawned, stepping gingerly down the ancient staircase and nodded a greeting to the hotel clerk.

"So, about that tea set…"

The clerk nodded, turning in deference, and a woman in a flowing emerald gown emerged to look up at Vexx. "Ah yes, our visitor from last night. The tea set, yes, set it out here and I'll take a look."

Vexx spread out the silver tea set. The woman picked up each piece, examining them carefully, and whistled in approval. "We do have many travellers coming through here, and I think we could do a nice side business with this. Let's see…" she thought for a moment, then named a figure.

Vexx considered it, shrugged, then extended his hand. The two smiled as they shook hands in agreement.

"A good deal! And so early in the morning," the hotel owner said, passing over the coins and shooting Vexx a smile. "I also heard you're interested in a job? I wonder, do you want to earn back last night's costs?"

"Absolutely. The name's Vexx White, ma'am, dungeoneer for hire. How can I help?"

"What a strong name for a young man such as your-self! And I've heard you travel with quite the company. Look, you want to earn back your lodging?" The hotel owner pointed out of the window at the decrepit barn. "We stable horses there when we get a lot of big caravans coming through. Or used to, anyway…there was an inci-dent with an exotic goods trader and a witch, and well, one thing led to another and it's haunted now."

"Haunted."

"Yeah, spirits of the damned and things of that nature. You know what I mean. A jar of trapped souls fell and they need some sort of eternal release. Honestly, this sort of thing happens more often than you'd think. Don't go into hotel work. You think it'd be easy, right? Just keep the beds cleaned? But this and that adds up, and before you know it…well, anyway, just deal with this haunting problem and we'll call it even for the night."

"Great. I think I can do it."

"The sooner, the better, I don't want this haunting business spreading into the rooms. The last thing we need are the screams of tortured souls keeping my guests up at night. Oh, and there's also a lot of spiders."

"Spiders?"

"Yeah. There was an infestation that just sort of, you know, grew. And now they're everywhere. So get rid of the spiders while you're at it."

"I see. And was that it?"

"That should do it."

Vexx grumbled, sticking one hand into his jumbled mess of a haircut. He examined the tea kettle for a moment. "Think I can try a cup?"

39

GHOSTS AND SPIDERS

Vexx felt fresh and ready for his new task. His spirits rose as he sipped a hot cup of green tea in the lobby. He raised a hand in greeting as Kaylin emerged and made her way over to him in another chair.

"I got us a job."

"Ooh, a quest?" Kaylin leaned in close and took an experimental sniff at Vexx's tea, her head close to his chest. "What's this? Tea?"

"Yeah…" Vexx found himself gazing at her neckline, then guiltily tore his eyes away. "Uh, I thought I might as well try it. Also, I wouldn't go so far as to call this a quest. Just an errand really—clearing out their barn out back."

The click of heels on wood drew their attention up. Shyola leaned on the curving staircase and raised an eyebrow as she stared down at them. "Up so soon, Master! Am I to understand we're shoveling stables now? I didn't endure centuries trapped in a book to engage in manual labor. Not unless it's…*pleasurable* labor."

"It isn't shoveling!" Vexx protested. "At least…it

mostly isn't. Look, there are spirits of the damned stuck in there. You might meet some old friends."

"Oh, why didn't you say so? If there are spirits of the damned, then I'm in," she said, joining them at the stable but remaining standing. "No time like the present, Master." She glanced over at Kaylin. "Still with us, I see, elf."

Kaylin frowned and opened her mouth to retort.

"Let's not start this again," Vexx cut in quickly. He slid the chair closer to the table and ushered them both out of the lobby. "Come on, it's just out back."

He stepped through the muddy ground behind the shoddy inn, past the stables where a farmer was leading a sow away and a traveller was brushing her horse, and approached the old storage shed. Vexx examined it for a moment.

"Well, it doesn't *look* haunted."

"Appearances can be deceiving, darling. I can smell their torment from here." Shyola licked her lips hungrily.

Vexx hesitated for a moment before he placed one hand on the shed door, then threw it open. The joints squealed as the door opened. Vexx squinted into the darkness before summoning a flame that lit the interior of the dusty shed, casting light in all corners. He saw movement, and as his eyes adjusted to the darkness, he realized that those shapes were gigantic spiders scurrying around in the shadows. Kaylin shrieked in his ear and clutched at his arm in terror. Vexx grimaced as he lurched away from her screeching.

"You didn't say anything about spiders!" Kaylin cried.

Vexx glanced back to see the elf running away. He sighed.

"Never fear, Master, the creatures of the night bother

me not," Shyola said, stepping into the shed. She slammed the sharp heel of her shoe down as a spider ran by, splattering its guts onto the floor. "Begone, spiders!" She slashed down, her whip cracking as it snapped beside another spider, bursting it apart. The succubus laughed as she snapped her whip at others, a few spiders scurrying past.

"Well, at least they aren't giant ones," Vexx said, stepping inside and casting his light in all directions. After his scrap with the rats, he figured he'd be careful about this, but aside from a few old, half-rotting saddles and spare wagon wheels, there seemed to be hardly anything inside the shed.

Vexx jumped when Shyola slammed her foot down and viciously ground the remains of an unlucky spider into the floor. "That seems to be the last one. The others got the message."

Vexx opened his mouth to speak, then felt a cool shiver, as if ice had been pressed into his body. It passed a moment later, but he continued to feel a strange, unearthly sensation. Shyola nodded as if in understanding.

"Now to those poor souls," she said, with a peculiar hint of sadness. "You were able to dominate me, Master, so I imagine your necromantic skills will allow you to release them. Just cast your energy out and commune with their souls. I will help you if you need it."

Vexx nodded, closing his eyes to better concentrate, and felt out the room with his magic. "I can sense you, lost ones. Speak to me, spirits," Vexx said, and then heard a tumult of a dozen voices.

"Doom, doom!"

"Curses of a thousand years upon—"

"There is no end! There is—"

"Flee this place, mortal, flee!"

"Your flesh will—"

Vexx held a hand up. "Whoa, slow down. One at a time. Sort it out yourselves, I can't see you in the spectral plane. Let me know when you're ready."

He stood there in silence, then felt an unearthly tug on his robes. Vexx kept his expression carefully blank. "Oh damned soul, what keeps you tied here?"

"My name is Armineus. I was a caravan guard and I was cursed by a witch to be tied to that copper pitcher. And it was a rotten business! She couldn't take a joke and went ahead—

"You had it coming!" Another spirit, presumably the witch, shouted angrily.

"Hold it," Vexx said, hand held up in the air. "I'll get to you, ma'am. Let me just sort out Armineus here." He paused, then opened one eye and looked over at Shyola. "Shy, grab that copper pitcher over there and sell it to a blacksmith. Make sure he smelts it—give him a good price, but make sure it gets done."

"Got it," she said, grabbing the pitcher, and Vexx closed both his eyes. He felt Armineus sigh in relief.

"Won't be long now, sir. Now, who's next?"

"It's me, Helga. The witch."

Vexx heard the grumbles of a half dozen other souls.

"She cursed us!"

"Alright, steady," Vexx replied. "How can we expel your soul?"

"The exotic goods dealer who disrespected me was bound to this realm—"

"You absolute—"

"You deserved it!" the witch screeched back, as the spirit of the exotic goods seller grumbled to himself. "Anyway, he has a son selling lacquerware and pottery just off Gourd Street. I want you to kill him."

"I'm not going to do that."

"He must suffer!"

Vexx sighed. "I could probably…break a few pots."

He winced at his lame compromise and fought the urge to fidget in the icy silence.

"That would be sufficient," the witch said. "See to it that you do. I can finally depart this realm."

"Great. Next?"

A FEW CONVERSATIONS LATER, Vexx opened his eyes to see Kaylin standing in the shed, shyly shuffling her feet beside the spare wagon wheels. "Sorry, Vexx. Those spiders just freaked me out."

"It's alright. Hey, can you do a favor for me? There's a stone mason on Tower Road. Tell him to make a grave marker that says Paulina Cooper. I'll put it beside Henry Cooper and these souls can have peace."

"Got it," Kaylin said, already heading out. Vexx closed his eyes once again, feeling himself growing impatient. *How many souls do I have left here? If I keep going at this pace, this could take all day.*

"Spirit of the damned, speak your piece and be quick," Vexx said.

"Nothing's tying me here," an elderly man's voice replied. "It's just that witch who—"

"Great," Vexx said, snapping his fingers as he released the spirit with his necromantic energies. He felt the absence of one of the spirits. "Next?"

"There is one thing that keeps me bound to this

mortal plane," came a rasping voice, tickling the edge of Vexx's consciousness. "My husband awaits me, far across the land, a journey of seventy and three days, hidden somewhere on distant Nyte Island. He must have the Goblet of Redemption, which is guarded by trolls on the Island of Sorrow, a journey of sixty and—"

"That seems like a whole thing," Vexx butted in. "I'm just going to go ahead and release you," he said, summoning his necromantic magic.

"Oh," the spirit said. "Well, I suppose you could just do—"

Vexx snapped his fingers, and the spirit departed the mortal realm. "Next!"

40

FAVORS FOR THE DEAD

The dungeoneers strolled through the streets of Western Cloudbury, their stomachs grumbling.

"Can we eat yet, Vexx?" Kaylin asked.

"Let's sell this first," he replied, patting his packet of erotic dryad art. "Plus, the potter is just over there. Ah, there he is," Vexx said, spotting a few huge earthenware pots set out for display. A thin, balding man was humming to himself as he polished a ceramic urn.

"Shy, can you distract him for a few moments?"

She snorted. "I don't think I need to answer that, Master," she said, sidling down the street, and attracting glances with every step. "Oh, yoohoo! Pottery man!"

Vexx snuck past, his cloak up and his eyes downcast, drifting through the market day crowd until he reached the giant pots out for display. He reached for a cudgel they'd picked up from the last batch of goblin corpses, glancing one way and the other. He almost dropped it as he was started by a voice behind him.

"What are you doing?" Kaylin asked loudly.

Vexx raised a finger to his mouth and looked over, eyes

bulging. "Shh! It's to release the last soul. Job's not over yet."

"Ohh…" she said slowly, much louder than he would have liked. Over the commotion of traffic, he heard the shop owner stammering something about mud mixing with water. Shyola's titter echoed around them. *Well, at least he'll be distracted. A half-naked succubus is perfect for that.*

Vexx gritted his teeth, feeling a moment of sympathy, but pushed it aside. *Gotta do what you gotta do,* he thought to himself, smashing the first pot. He stepped over to the next one, slamming the cudgel in, whirling around and slamming the head into the last giant pot on display. *That should do it. Rest in peace, you malicious old ghoul.*

"Hey, what's going on?"

"Never mind that, you cutie," Shyola's voice echoed over the shopkeeper's squeals. "How about you and me—"

"My pots!"

"Let's get out of here," Vexx snapped, already hurrying down the street, Kaylin running beside him. They darted through an alley, then backtracked a block before sauntering down the street without a care in the world. He nodded at the inn just down the street, as they passed a cart loaded down with lumber. "We'll finish the deal and then get lunch. Sound good?"

Kaylin sniffed. "I didn't get into dungeoneering to smash people's pots."

"Well, *you* didn't do a thing," Vexx pointed out, pushing the rickety inn door open and stepping inside. He blinked in surprise, taking in Shyola, who was leisurely reclining on a chair, her long legs draped over one of the arm rests. The clerk did not look happy about that, frowning silently from behind the desk. "How did you get here first?"

Shy shrugged. "I don't know what took you so long. Did the elf slow you down?"

"Well, never mind that," Vexx said, approaching the clerk. "Is the mistress of the house around? We've finished expelling the spirits from your shed."

"And the spiders?"

Vexx turned at the voice and was greeted with the sight of the innkeeper approaching. She smiled as she slid on one long leather glove and then another.

"And the spiders. Are you going to check on it?"

"Of course," she said, gesturing for Vexx to follow as she stepped outside. "Let's hope you're right. Business is going to be booming soon, and I'll need as much space as I can get."

"Speaking of business," Vexx added, hurrying over to follow and pulling out his collection of erotic dryad art. "Would you or your guests be in the market for this?"

41

THE PICKPOCKET

"There's just no appreciation for art anymore," Vexx complained as they walked through the dusty streets of Cloudbury. "I can't believe the innkeeper scrunched her nose up like that. It's like she thought I was trying to sell her a half-filled chamber pot!" He cursed as a boy bumped into him. "Watch where you go, kid!"

"They're quaint, simple people here," Shyola observed. "Why, in the flesh warrens of a lower hell, such pictures would seem positively wholesome. How much money do we have, Master?"

"Well, we have a bit," Vexx said, feeling for his coin purse. "But not nearly…hey!" He blinked, patted his robes in bewilderment, then spun around to see the boy darting into an alley. "Hey! After that kid!"

"Why?" Kaylin asked, as Vexx stormed past. Shyola was faster on the uptake, sprinting forward and matching pace with Vexx as they rounded the corner, running through the alleyway. Vexx hesitated a moment and skidded to a stop.

He cursed as mud splattered on the hem of his robe. "Which way?"

"There!" Shyola said, hooking a sharp left and leaping over a pile of ruined furniture. "I see the little scoundrel!"

"Right behind you!" Vexx called out as he skirted around the furniture and sprinted to catch up. He saw the boy now and tried to make sense of his movements. The boy darted from alley to alley, then he turned a corner and they were faced with two options.

Shyola took a passageway to the left, and Vexx took one to the right, looking to trap the pickpocket in the warrens. He slowed, coming to an intersection, and then heard the snap of a whip. Vexx groaned. *Don't kill the kid, you crazy demon. I just want my stuff back!*

He perked back up as he heard the panicked stamping of feet and turned to see the boy running straight at him. Behind him, Shyola's echoing laughter chased him onward.

"I will steal your soul, child!" She cracked her whip and laughed again. "An eternity of torment!"

"Hold up," Vexx said, raising his hand as the boy glanced up in fright, slowing and coming to a stop. "Don't get any ideas. I'll be wanting my pouch back."

"Ah, come on," the boy said, glancing back fearfully at Shyola. She had reached them now and came to a halt, her whip still glowing brightly in the dim light of the alley. "I don't want any trouble," he said, trembling as he tossed Vexx's coin purse to him. "I'm just trying to get by."

"Yeah, yeah, it's fine," Vexx muttered. "Take it easy, Shy."

The succubus made a sound of disapproval, but said nothing more as Vexx rummaged through his coin purse. *Everything's there.* He looked back at the nervous pickpocket, who seemed to be trying to inconspicuously inch away.

"Hey, think I can go, fella?"

"Not just yet." Vexx crouched down to eye level with the boy. "Who do you sell your merchandise to?"

"Ah, you're kidding me," the boy grumbled, fidgeting in his pockets. "I can't tell you that."

"How much is your soul worth?" Vexx asked, then glanced up at Shyola. The boy grimaced.

"Alright, fine. I'll take you to a guy I sell most of my goods to. Just don't make a big scene or anything, alright?"

"Me? Of course not!" Vexx said, moving out of the pickpocket's way. "We're just new in town, looking for work and a place to sell anything we might come across. We end up with a lot of second-hand merchandise," Vexx added, patting the goblin cudgel that still hung on his belt.

"Oh, you're dungeoneers!" the boy blinked. "Well, why didn't you say so? Don Kordo loves dungeoneers. Says they'll do the work that no one else is stupid enough to do."

Vexx grimaced. *There might be some truth to that.* He waved his hand. "Lead on, kid."

42

THE SLUMS OF CLOUDBURY

"I've been looking all over for you, Vexx!"

Vexx turned to look through the crowds of Cloud-bury's street and waved a hand over. "Hey, Kaylin!"

The elf skipped through the crowds to join them, raising an eyebrow as she noticed they were following the boy through Cloudbury's streets. "Was this your pick-pocket? You're not chasing him very quickly. Did you get tired?"

"No, Kaylin," Vexx said with a sigh. "He says he knows some people that might have a few jobs for us. As you can see, everything else is turning out dry."

"Working with thieves now?"

The boy slowed, raising a finger to his lips. "Keep it down, elf! Don Kordo doesn't like that kind of talk. We work in *procurement*, and he works in *delivery*. Just keep that straight and we won't have any problems. Otherwise..." he shrugged, then resumed making his way through the slums of Western Cloudbury.

"It'll be fine," Vexx said, and the party of dungeoneers followed the boy through the stinking shanty town that bordered the town wall. *I hope, anyway. I've never really been to this part of town. Never even had any reason to even pass through here.*

He nodded down at a beggar who appeared to only have one arm. Kaylin looked on curiously as he rattled a bowl with a couple coppers and one tooth inside it. *We're not too far off from you, friend.* Vexx straightened, noting a dilapidated but somehow dignified-looking house amidst the chaos of the slums. *But perhaps our luck is looking up.*

An orc strolled out the front floor, looking aimless at first, then stood stock still and frowned at their approach as they neared the house.

"Hey, Brundisio," the pickpocket said in a familiar tone. "Just some procurers looking for work."

The orc grunted, his hand tapping the haft of an axe resting on his belt. He had two axes on either side and he had another double-headed one strapped to his back. *A berserker, then. Not someone I'd care to tangle with.* Vexx nodded at the orc.

"Just mind your manners," Brundisio grunted from between his fangs. "Make Don Kordo unhappy, and I'll gut you myself. You keep an eye on them, Gary."

"Sure thing," the boy said, waving them over as he put a hand on the ornate wooden door. It gleamed with a flickering orange light. "It has a magical enchantment on it," Gary explained. "It tingles a bit, but as long as it's opened slowly, you'll be fine. Don't rush in, though. It'll zap you to dust," he said, slowly creaking the door open.

"Ah, my boy," came a booming voice from inside. "Is your day of pickpocketing over already? Why, the sun is still high up in the sky."

"I found something even better, Don Kordo," the boy

said, making room for the dungeoneers. "Some procurers. Dungeoneers, actually! And they're looking for work!"

Vexx stepped into the house, the half-rotted floor creaking beneath him, a smile plastered on his face. Seated at a desk was a fat half-orc, his stringy black hair brushed to the side, a contemplative expression on his face. He drummed thick fingers on the desk, a massive oak table littered with jewelled skulls, trinkets, magically enchanted daggers, silver and gold pendants, and a few glowing potions. It looked like the hoard of a dragon.

"Well, well," Don Kordo boomed out. "Plenty of people looking for work. The old beggar down the street is looking for work. What separates you from the rest?"

"We know how to handle ourselves in a fight," Vexx said. "I trained in the Magical Academy at Fallanden," he added, snapping his fingers. A flame emerged, Don Kordo frowned disapprovingly, and Vexx dispelled it sheepishly.

"Don't do that again," Don Kordo rumbled. "So you're a mage, then. I don't see those very often. Hmm…" his eyes flicked over to Shyola and Kaylin. "You two, I can find work for," he said with a chortle. "But it wouldn't be in the procuring business. You, though…" he blinked a few times, as if trying to figure Vexx out. "Just who the hell are you, anyway?"

"Vexx White, dungeoneer for hire. These are my associates, Kaylin and Shyola. They're *dungeoneers*, Don Kordo, and that's the work we're looking for."

"Hmm…Brundisio!" Don Kordo shouted, leaning back. A moment later, the door opened, the orc berserker squinting at the dungeoneers suspiciously.

"Any trouble, boss?"

"No trouble. That job tonight at Vestrual's Lumber Company. You know, the one we had to scrap?"

"Three man job, boss," Brundisio said with a touch of fear. "Ole Arren's out with the leg wound, and that means just me and the new guy Kallan. And you know how he—"

"Never mind all that," Don Kordo said, waving his hand dismissively. "Kallan can stay back. Take these three along with you. The job's back on," he said with a grin.

"What job, exactly?" Vexx asked hesitantly. He wasn't too keen about working with this Don Kordo character in the first place, but the good people of Cloudbury weren't looking to hire him, so he had to take what he could get.

I just don't want to kill any innocents. I draw the line there. Shy wouldn't mind, but Kaylin definitely would. We'll back out if it comes to that.

"Oh, don't worry yourselves, dungeoneers," the half-orc said. "This is a milk run. You might not know, given that you're not from the slums around here, but there are all sorts of protection rackets and shady dealings going on with the lumber mills outside Cloudbury. It's a big business here, and the guard looks away if you pass them a few coins. The thing is…we had a deal with Gallagher Lumber Emporium. I won't bother you with the details, but they've been having some run-ins with thugs hired by Vestrual's Lumber Company—and it's time we put a stop to it."

"Great," Vexx muttered. "A gang fight over lumber."

"Hey, don't knock it," Don Kordo rumbled. "Plenty of money in trees. Besides, most of the time, we guard against goblin raids. People love us then."

"Alright, well…" Vexx glanced at Shyola, who seemed indifferent, though she was studying a jewelled skull with an air of intense fascination, and then looked over at Kaylin. The elf kept her face carefully blank, but gave Vexx a slight nod. He sighed, nodding to himself as well. "We're in."

"Course you are," Don Kordo huffed. "It's good money. Brundisio will show you the ropes. The job starts at dusk."

"Before all that, though," Vexx said, reaching into his robes. Brundisio snarled. "Easy, easy, just trying to sell this," Vexx added, then slowly placed Naruan's collection of art on the table. "Can I interest you in some erotic dryad art?"

The half-orc snorted. "Hell no. I deal in the real stuff out back," he said, jerking a thumb back to an inn, just visible through a window. *So that's what those sounds were,* Vexx thought to himself. "I don't need this. Find someone else to peddle this to."

Vexx sighed. "Well, it was worth a shot. I'm told it can be very valuable to collectors."

"This look like an art gallery to you? Brundisio, take these three and tell them the plan. I've got a criminal enterprise to run here. Gary, tell me you found more than just these dungeoneers here—I got a wagon leaving at dusk for Oerchenbrach and I want more goods on it. Dump what you got, then get your grubby little fingers back out there!"

43

THROWING AXES

Brundisio readied an axe, carefully targeting a mark he'd chipped into a tree in the forests outside Cloudbury. With a grunt, he threw it forward, watching it fly end over end before it buried itself in the wood.

Kaylin clapped her hands together. "A fine throw!"

Brundisio grinned as he walked over to the tree and with a grunt, he gripped the two throwing axes that were also lodged into it. A thin trickle of sap dribbled down from where they had landed.

"I still don't think you should practice on trees, though," she added. "They're living beings, you know."

He snorted, ripping one axe out and holstering it, then wrenching the second one out of the tree. "Who cares about trees? Besides, the logging companies all around here chop them down by the hundreds."

"There's a purpose to it, though," Kaylin said. "You make your buildings from them. Elves make their bows from trees as well. But this just causes damage to them for no end."

"There's a purpose," Brundisio grunted. "Practicing my

throwing axes. There's a fight on tonight, and your puny lives might depend on it. I figure you'll be as useless as Kallan here."

"Hey!" Kallan whined in his nasally tone. The scrawny slum fighter had insisted in accompanying them to the forest, even after Brundisio had made it clear he wasn't included in this job. Vexx was beginning to see why. Kallan might be as impressive a fighter as any, but he was already starting to grate on him. *Besides, I doubt he's nearly as good as he claims.*

"Don't even start," Brundisio growled. "I remember that last fight we were in with Ole Arren, trying to take over that warehouse. Barely light at all, and I know how terrible you humans are in the dark at the best of times, and then Arren takes a wild swing to the leg."

"That wasn't me," Kallan protested.

"Oh, I'm pretty sure it was." Brundisio paused. "But never mind that. Just practice like I'm doing, and be careful with your swings. You never know, the same thing might happen to you, and you might not be so forgiving as Ole Arren."

"Fine," Kallan grunted, turning to slash sullenly the nearest tree with his huge broadsword, his swing sending bits of wood flying through the air. Kaylin frowned at the sight but said nothing.

"Are you going to practice?" Brundisio asked, readying another throw.

Vexx shrugged. "My fireballs might burn down the whole forest. Besides, using magic really wears a person out. I'll be ready, have no fear."

Brundisio grunted, looking over at Shyola. "And you, succubus?"

"Practice?" Shy laughed. "Darling, I have eons of practice. If I practiced draining a soul, why, I don't know that I'd stop. And my whip?" She lunged forward, snapping it into existence, the reddish-orange magical whip slashed straight through a tree. It slid to the side, the rest of the group scrambling away as it tilted to the side and then collapsed on the ground. "Yes, it still works," she added in the silence, the whip fizzling away into nonexistence.

"Damn," Brundisio said, eyebrows raised. "You should be your own logging company."

"Ah, but I prefer adventuring with a cute young Master instead," she said, placing a delicate hand on Vexx's shoulder. She grinned over at him. "For now, anyway…"

The silence lingered.

Kaylin coughed. "I'd like to try those throwing axes, if you don't mind, Brundisio."

"Oh?" He shrugged. "I don't see why not." He twirled one around, handing it haft-first to the elf. "The tricky part is getting the axe head to land just where you want it, instead of it just bouncing off. Try that tree over there," he said, pointing over.

Kaylin gripped the throwing axe, grounding her feet, and nodded. "The one just to the left of Kallan?" she asked, as wood ships flew in the air from the scrawny fighter's sword strokes.

"Yes, the one I've been practicing on. Try and hit the mark in the center."

"Got it," Kaylin said, pulling it back, then flung it and excitedly fidgeted as it spun end over end. The axe head lodged with a solid thunk into Kallan's head just as he reared back for another strike. For a long moment, there was a stunned silence. Then, Kallan toppled bonelessly into the ground.

"Oh shit," Vexx muttered.

Brundisio let out a long sigh. "That's a problem. He wasn't even supposed to be here. Still…" he stepped forward, examining the corpse.

"Whoops…" Kaylin whispered, shrugging her shoulders.

"You're a natural," the orc said, kicking the fighter's motionless leg. "Ah, I couldn't stand him, anyway." He looked up at the sky. "Another hour until dusk, maybe. He was supposed to guard our wagon down the road."

Vexx nodded. They'd taken a wagon the short distance outside of Cloudbury. It was walking distance, but Brundisio had pointed out that a quick getaway wagon was essential if the situation turned sour. *And given our luck…*

Vexx cracked his fingers and strode forward. "You know, Brundisio, maybe I *will* get some practice in."

"Eh?"

The dungeoneer kneeled beside the fallen slum fighter. He had a pallid complexion, even before his untimely death, and his face looked normal enough given the circumstances. There was just the small issue of the axe sticking out the back of his head. Vexx placed his hand above the man, pressing down with a surge of necromantic energies, and felt the corpse twitch under his hands and groan as it began to move.

"Shit! What!" Brundisio stumbled backward. "Kallan, you thick-headed oaf, how did you survive that?"

Shyola chuckled. "He's not alive, silly, he's undead. Vexx is a necromancer. He does this sort of thing all the time."

Brundisio stammered a series of orc curses, then shook his head. "Necromancy. It's unnatural. You never mentioned that."

"People judge," Vexx said, stepping back as Kallan

clambered to his feet. The undead fighter blinked, one arm reaching back, fingers clawing at the axe head. "No, Zombie Kallan, don't touch it." Vexx looked at the others. "I'm still not entirely sure how it works, but I don't want him to sever the connection," he said, concentrating on the flickering yellow and green energies just visible between his hand and Zombie Kallan's skull.

"You mean I can't get my axe back?" Brundisio asked after a moment.

"You have two others," Vexx pointed out, then looked Zombie Kallan in the face. "Look, be a good boy and look after the wagon. We'll be by later tonight."

Zombie Kallan grunted something, then shambled off into the undergrowth, a branch snapping as the haft of the axe broke it.

"He'll be fine," Vexx added. *Probably*.

Brundisio sniffed, having apparently recovered from the death and undeath of his former companion. "I'll be wanting that axe back later. But, for now…maybe we should end our little practicing session here."

44

VESTRUAL'S LUMBER COMPANY

The dungeoneers laid in wait just outside the clearing around Vestrual's Lumber Company, watching as the lanterns of the night guards bobbed up and down as they continued their regular patrol. Vexx pulled his robes closer around him in an attempt to ward off the coolness of the air in the lower Lifeless Hills. He fidgeted, the chill mixed with the growing tension made him restless. He watched them in silence, and they seemed like a motley assortment of characters with no common uniform. Vexx crept over to Brundisio.

"You're sure they're hired thugs?"

"Oh, sure I'm sure," the orc replied, pointing a long green finger toward one lantern. "I even know some of them. You see that orc there? We practically grew up together. He's Thoran, and he's been a Lowrie Boy since about ten. That fellow just past him is the same."

"A...what?"

"A Lowrie Boy. Yeah, that's the gang this lumber company hired. There's about a dozen gangs in the slums, and Don Kordo..." Brundisio winced. "Well, let's just say with Ole Arren wounded and Kallan put down, he doesn't have a lot of foot soldiers left. Truth be told, this is probably our last chance to avoid being taken over by one of the bigger gangs. I hope you can handle yourselves."

"Sure," Vexx said, "though we're just dungeoneers for hire, you understand. So let me get this straight. We're striking back for your lumber company, setting a few fires, maybe stealing some of their lumber if it looks like we can get away with it, for Don Kordo to make a bit of a profit on the side and boost his gang's reputation."

"Right," Brundisio nodded.

"So we don't need to kill them all."

The orc bared his fangs. "You see a way to do all that without killing them all?"

Vexx pursed his lips. "I think…maybe I do. Think you can lure some of them off?"

"What, me do all the heavy lifting here? Face all the risks?"

"It's that or fighting them head on." Vexx gritted his teeth, already regretting taking on this assignment. *Who knew the odds would be so heavily stacked against us? We have surprise on our side, at least. That might just be enough.*

"Gentlemen," Shyola whispered from above. The dungeoneer and the orc gasped, then shifted aside as she dropped soundlessly from the tree above. "Sounds like you're looking for a sneaky succubus to suck out some souls," she purred. "I'm your woman. Let me at them."

Vexx cracked a smile. "Sure thing, Shy. Will you distract a few of them for us, Brundisio?"

The orc nodded. "I'll make some goblin calls. They're always prowling around up here, and I'm sure they'll take a look. Once I hear fighting down below or see a fire, I'll kill my way through them."

Vexx nodded as the orc prowled his way through the underbrush. They waited in silence until he heard a few distant rattles and clacks that sounded like a patrol of goblins. A few of the lanterns jerked to the side, distant shouts emerging from the lumber building. After a moment, four more lights emerged from within.

Vexx cursed. There are even more around? This is insane!

"I'll make my way closer," Shyola said, creeping her way forward. The elf peeked her head up, ears sticking out through the undergrowth.

"Vexx, where's she going?" she asked.

"She's going to sneak up and take out some of the guards," he whispered back. "Shush."

"I can do that! I'm sneaky too!" Kaylin hissed from a nearby bush. Vexx held a hand up as if to silence her, and saw a lantern twitch in the distance.

"Did you hear that?" a voice asked.

"Hear what?"

The silence lingered for a minute as everyone remained motionless, with only distant goblin sounds and rustling, as some of the guards made their way up the nearest hills. Finally, the lantern moved aside.

"Nothing, I guess," the voice said, sounding a bit sheepish. If there was a reply, Vexx couldn't hear it. He waited a while longer before turning to glare at Kaylin.

"Not so loud," he whispered.

"Sorry. But Vexx, I can be sneaky! I'm an elf, we're supposed to be good at that."

"Supposed to, but…" he sighed. "Fine, show me how sneaky you are. There are two guards on this side," Vexx continued, pointing over at the lanterns nearby. "Shyola can take one down and you can get the other."

"Oh, I'll be so silent about it," Kaylin muttered. "Everyone's going to know just how silent I am. Hey, where's Shyola?"

Vexx pointed over to where a dark shape was slowly sneaking behind one of the guards on patrol. Kaylin cursed, then hurried over toward the other one, branches snapping under her feet. Vexx sighed to himself. *Even so, I have to admit that I would probably be even louder. I don't really go much for sneaking.* Vexx glanced over into the distance, where Brundisio must be leading a few of the Lowrie Boys away. *Still, there's no one better at setting fires. In and out, then back to Don Kordo. Couldn't be easier.*

45

SNEAKY DUNGEONEERS

The first lantern swung wildly as a dark shape leaped forward, an accompanying burst of spectral energy radiating outward. The light from the lantern fell and extinguished itself on the ground, casting the surroundings back into blackness. Vexx strode forward, hearing slurping and cracking sounds mixed with Shyola's moans of delight. He glanced up at the next lantern just as it fell, getting a glimpse of Kaylin behind an orc, her blade slicing across its neck. The orc guard staggered to the side, blood spurting out, and then they were left in darkness as well.

Using his other senses more than his terrible night vision, Vexx almost bumped into Shyola, her burp breaking the silence. There were no other guards around, at least, though for all Vexx knew, a few could still be inside the lumber mill. Shy moaned again, louder this time, ignoring Vexx's shushing.

"Oh, the hopes and dreams of that one!" Shyola declared. "It's so rare that you find a thug with aspirations like that! He wanted to be a singer, you know, to hit the nightclubs of Fallanden. But he never tried! He never tried, boys and girls, and that truly is a sad thing...it left such a deliciously poignant taste in my mouth. Mmm... but let that be a lesson to you, you young creatures. Pursue your dreams! He was thirty-eight and never truly admitted to others, much less himself, that singing was what he really wanted to do with his life. No, one thing led to another, and he just drifted along with the tides. From one gang to another, just a foot soldier, a thug to help satisfy other people's dreams. He thought he was different, he did, as so many other souls do. Ah, anyway...it was good stuff. Cloudbury scum is a lot tastier than I would have imagined."

Kaylin had crept over, casting a puzzled look at the succubus. "You know, it's quicker if you just knife them," she muttered.

"Silly elf, you need to treasure the pleasures in life. Particularly when it's being extinguished. Ooh, I'm on such a high right now," the succubus continued, almost skipping as she paced through the clearing on her way to the lumber mill, a broad smile on her face. Vexx hissed after her to slow down, then rose to his feet.

"Come on, Kaylin."

The two dungeoneers followed along, hearing a sudden shriek from inside, and then the sounds of glass breaking and furniture clattering. Vexx rushed in as he heard Shyola moan in satisfaction, dodging just in time as the succubus flung a drained corpse against the wall, collapsing on top of a bucket and mop. He looked back to see Shyola wiping her mouth. She was in a room littered with papers, discarded glasses, and various boxes. It seemed to be the main office of the lumber mill, and based on the chairs and bottles scattered around, the place where the night guards did most of their drinking.

"That one was unsatisfying," she announced as Vexx entered the open lumber mill. "Like eating pea soup after a wonderful cake. The rest of the mill is clear, though. The fools are rushing about up in the woods chasing after Brundisio. Shall I leave the burning to you, Master?"

"Yes," he said, pacing through the empty and dimly lit warehouse floor. There were a few stacks of lumber laying around, and Vexx slowed to look at them, thinking of the bonus they could make if they were to steal some of them. *And with a wagon not far off...*

"What are you thinking?" Kaylin asked, an arrow nocked to her bow. She had taken a defensive position beside one of the windows facing up into the hills. The guards had likely just been there mere minutes ago. Vexx glanced around to see a wooden ladder leading up to rafters, a few unattended saws, and various other tools and workbenches beside the walls.

"I'm thinking we can steal some of these," Vexx said, tapping the lumber. "As much as we can stuff into the wagon."

"Ambitious," Shyola purred from across the warehouse. "I love it, Master. Anything you require of me?"

"Just keep watch and take out any guards who come back," Vexx thought, already summoning Zombie Kallan. *He's a bit down the road, but even undead he should be able to manage the horse. I hope.* "Kaylin, help me stack some of these planks by the door. Zombie Kallan and I will load it up."

"Sure thing," she said, as they began piling up the smaller planks. "Is that clatter the wagon coming?" she asked, her ears twitching, but all Vexx could make out were the fake goblin grunts and rattles from the hills nearby. "I guess so," he said, huffing as he hurried to get the lumber readied. "The guards are sure to notice. Get in position by the window—we'll handle the rest," he said, pushing open the huge creaking doors of the lumber mill. There was little point in keeping quiet now. He heaved both of the huge doors open, then stood panting in the open, finally hearing the clack of hooves and wagon wheels.

He stood up, spotting the faint glow of the wagon's lantern as it clattered over. Vexx waved his hands, for what little good it will do him. "Over here!" he hissed. The wagon was in the clearing now, approaching the open gate. "Load this up!"

"Oh, Master?"

Vexx turned at Shyola's call. She was at the ground floor window, and Vexx saw Kaylin clambering up to the rafters and hurrying over to a window on the second story. *A better firing position, I suppose.*

"What's going on?" Vexx asked, raising his voice louder than he would have liked just to be heard over the increasing noises in the hills. *Brundisio is really putting on quite the performance out there.*

"It's Brundisio," Shyola said, making way to him just as the orc leaped through the window. "And that's not all! The guards are running back, and there are—"

"Goblins!" Brundisio shouted as he rose to his feet. "A whole pack of them!"

46

CHAOS IN THE LUMBER MILL

Vexx rushed over to the side door they had entered, making sure to check all exits and entrances. With this one covered, there was only the ground floor window and the main loading bay. He saw a few guards running back in the distance, and even a few smaller shapes he half-recognized as goblins.

A raid right now? Who should I focus on? His fingers twitched, then he readied a burst of flames. *I'll blaze a wall in front of the door,* Vexx thought, already firing his flames. *It's about time we burned the place down and left, anyway.* The grass in a half-circle around the door was burning away now, along with the edge of the warehouse. It wouldn't stop everyone, but it would sure give them something to think about. Vexx turned, hurrying back to the loading bay doors, noting that Brundisio had joined Zombie Kallan. Together, they were sliding lumber into the wagon.

"Good thinking," the orc grunted when he spotted Vexx. "Keep the bastards off us and we'll get out with plenty of profit to boot."

"Right," Vexx said, rushing to the window. "Just hurry!"

He glanced out, to see Shyola out in the open, laughing as she slashed her whip at a Lowrie Boy. The man collapsed mid-charge, the whip severing him in half, and a few others hesitated. Then one of them staggered, the dark outline of an arrow jutting out from its shoulder.

"I don't need your help, elf!" Shyola shouted. A few other Lowrie Boys arrived, one with a gleaming robe that shone with an inner light as if enchanted with magic. As Vexx watched, he raised a gleaming staff, and he felt a sinking feeling inside as a sparkling missile fired up into the night sky.

"Vexx, they have a mage!" Shyola called out from the second story, another shot flying just wide of the mage. The mage fired a burst of light into the sky, the light exploding in a shimmering display, its brilliance illuminated both the ground below and in all directions. In the distance, Vexx could make out a swarm of goblins rushing forward.

"Oh, great," Brundisio gasped out, joining him at the window. "They'll draw in reinforcements!"

"The Lowrie Boys?" Vexx asked, then blinked. "Are you done loading the wagon?" He turned to look back, seeing Zombie Kallan balancing a huge tree trunk on his shoulder, forcing it into the wagon.

"No, I don't know what your necromancy does, but he's not holding back. Mumbled something like 'he's got the rest.' Most useful Kallan's ever been. But we need to leave."

"That we do," Vexx said, firing a fireball as the Lowrie Boys began encircling Shyola, one lunging forward with a spear. He collapsed to the ground, shrieking as Vexx's fireball burned against his leather armor. "Shy, get out of there! We're leaving!"

Shy turned, taking a few steps forward. Then the mage pointed his staff forward, firing a blue bolt that burst on her left leg, tendrils of ice freezing it in place. She glanced up, immobile, struggling to move. "Master! Help!"

Vexx grimaced, firing a fireball at the mage, who deflected it with a wave of frost magic that sent it sputtering into the air, only to disappear into nothingness. *Frost mages are such cold-blooded assholes,* Vexx thought, firing a small firebolt that exploded on Shyola's leg. She gasped, then lurched forward as Vexx cleared the window. Shyola leaped in, rolling into the floor, then gingerly rubbed at her reddened leg.

"Ooh, it's so tingly! He almost gave me frostbite back there. You'll warm me up later, yes?"

Vexx roughly dragged her aside just as another frost bolt soared past. "Get to the wagon," he grunted, clambering back to his feet. "Kaylin, get out of there!" he shouted, firing a burst of flames into the corner of the lumber mill. "I'm going to burn it down!"

"Just a second," she shouted, still loosing arrows from the second story window. "They're moving around the barn. Goblins right behind. Ah!"

"Kaylin?" Vexx paused a moment from setting fires, rushing over to another corner of the warehouse, barely sparing a glance to see Zombie Kallan, Shyola, and Brundisio leading the laden wagon away. "Kaylin?"

He fired away in the corner, then turned back—to see a wave of ice washing over the flames he had set, already dying away. "Damn it!"

"Got him!" Kaylin shouted from above. "Just winged him, but—"

Snarling forms burst through the window—a pair of goblins. They whirled toward Vexx just as he backed away, firing a fireball that exploded in between them and slammed them against the wall. Then he kept firing, fireballs exploding left and right, shooting almost at random in every direction.

Just you try and extinguish that, asshole, he thought triumphantly, backing away and resting against the ladder, trying to get his stamina back. He breathed in deeply, then choked on the spreading smoke. "Kaylin! Get down from there!"

Vexx waited a moment, then clambered up halfway, looking over. Kaylin wasn't by the window any longer. The only thing left of her was a couple arrows and a small pool of blood.

47

THROUGH THE FLAMES

"Vexx, get out of there!" Shyola shouted from the distance, and Vexx shook his head to clear it, coughing from the smoke. There was no time. Vexx slid down the ladder and landed hard on the ground. He saw blurred shapes around him and heard the savage snarling as goblins tussled with Lowrie Boys in the burning warehouse, but they were none of his concern. He lurched forward, eyes focused on the hangar bay doors, staggering forward and then breaking into a run as he passed through a half-dozen struggling figures. Two others blocked his path, Lowie Boys by the look of them, and he shot a fireball forward to knock one down and send the other reeling away. Vexx leaped over the fallen Lowrie Boy, and then he was out into the cool mountain air, turning to see the fully laden wagon waiting beside the burning lumber mill.

Shyola, Zombie Kallan, and Brundisio stood around it in a loose cordon, fending off attacking goblins and Lowrie Boys. As Vexx approached, Brundisio leaped forward with a wild slash of his double-headed axe, ramming two goblins full in the chest. He rested it on his shoulder, waving Vexx over.

"Let's go!"

"But Kaylin," Vexx panted, glancing around. Then, he heard a thud on the wagon up above, and looked up to see that Kaylin had landed on the lumber pile.

"I ran across the roof," she said in a rush, nocking an arrow and quickly loosing it at a charging goblin brandishing a heavy flail.

"Get the horse moving," Vexx shouted up at her, just as the horse gave a panicked whinny, and Kaylin rushed over to settle into the wagon driver's seat. She slapped the reins and the wagon began rolling forward. A spear sliced through the air and Vexx dodged aside just in time. He suppressed a sigh of relief at the close call.

A group of goblins surged out of the burning warehouse and Vexx blasted them away with strong bursts of flames, and as one stumbled forward, Brundisio tossed his throwing axe to catch it in the head. He leaned down next to it, yanked it out of the goblin's skull, and ran to catch up to the wagon. Vexx followed close behind, flanking the wagon as it rattled along the dirt road. Is it going to be like this all the way to Cloudbury?

Vexx glanced left and right, seeing goblins hounding them from the sides, but at least no sign of the Lowrie Boys. I guess they must have died or ran off, Vexx thought, though that was little relief. He turned to look at Brundisio as they jogged along.

"Think the Lowrie Boys have had it?"

He shook his head quickly. "They're a big gang, and I know they have hideouts in the area. Reinforcements will be around soon."

"So much for a milk run," Vexx snapped, now keeping pace alongside the wagon. Zombie Kallan was out ahead of them, clearing the way with his broadsword, the goblins keeping their distance. Then one lunged forward and plunged its scimitar into Kallan's back, and as he turned back, two others seized the opportunity to leap forward. Their spears and swords impaled him clean through, but still, the undead fighter struggled, grabbing one of them by the arm. The goblin shrieked as the others dashed away, looking up in horror as the wagon rolled on, crushing both him and Zombie Kallan beneath it.

Brundisio slowed, and instinctively, Vexx slowed with him, keeping his attention on the sides. "Let's go!" Vexx snapped, reaching for a magical potion and popping the cork open, never once taking his eyes off the shifting movement in the forest beside the road.

"Just getting my axe back," he grunted, waiting until the wagon rolled by. Then he knelt by the corpse of Kallan and pulled his throwing axe from the back of the fighter's head. "Nice knowing you, buddy," he muttered, rushing back up to Vexx. Shyola's whip cracked on the other side of the wagon, but Vexx wasn't too worried about her, especially since she kept laughing and cackling.

She only gets quiet when she's in trouble. Besides, she'd call for help if she needs it.

"Can we go any faster, Kaylin?" Vexx asked, returning to the front of the overloaded wagon.

"The horse is going as fast as it can," she said, spurring the poor beast on once more. "Did you stuff half the forest in here?"

"It'll be worth it at the end," Brundisio panted, keeping pace beside Vexx.

"Did you tell Kallan that too?" Vexx muttered.

"Ah, who cares about Kallan? All that matters—"

A frost bolt soared out of the darkness beside the road, freezing a wagon wheel in an instant, rocking the wagon back and forth as it slowed and came to a stop. The horse whinnied as it slid to the side—then rocked back into place, immobile.

"Which one of you idiots thought to mess with the Lowrie Gang?" a voice called out, and then Vexx saw the gleaming robes of the mage appear from the side, followed by a half-dozen fighters in leather armor.

"The name's Vexx White, and I'll have your head, you icy bitch," Vexx replied, flames sizzling from his fingertips, suddenly grateful he'd drank the last of his magic potion.

"Oh, a fire mage," the man replied, scowling in the distance. He must have been in his thirties, with a jagged scar along one cheek and closely cropped brown hair. Up close, Vexx saw blood splotch and tear in his robe where Kaylin's arrow must have taken him. "How original," he sneered. "I'm Barnabus Lowrie, and my big brother will be along shortly. Though I don't plan on leaving any of you alive until then."

Brundisio cursed beside Vexx. "That's not good," he said in a low voice. "Maybe we can—"

Barnabus whipped his staff forward, firing a frost bolt just as Vexx dove into the dirt road, rolling and quickly coming to his feet. Vexx fired fireball after fireball at the man, one wild shot catching an archer beside him and another fizzling away into nothingness even as it hit him directly. Vexx paused, frowning in puzzlement, but Barnabus just laughed and patted his clothing.

"My anti-magic robe," he explained. "Nothing a pauper like you could afford in a thousand years, but when you head the Lowrie Boys..." he shrugged, then pointed his staff forward. "After them!"

The Lowrie Boys charged forward, one of them catching Kaylin's arrow on an oaken shield, as Vexx shot firebolt after firebolt. Shyola leaped forward, slashing her whip into a charging man's leg, and severing it entirely. The man stumbled screaming to the ground, and she dove in, draining his soul as he struggled against her. Three of them locked shields together, hemming in Vexx as he backed away, blocking his fireballs. One the shields was knocked askew, and a thrown axe hurtled into the gap, catching one in the neck.

The man's eyes widened as he stumbled to the ground, and then Brundisio charged forward, smashing a second man's shield into kindling with a heavy strike of his double-headed axe. Vexx followed it up with a fireball, then blasted away the other gang member, who lowered his shield in a panic.

Barnabus cursed from behind, his attention split between firing frost bolts at Brundisio and dodging arrows from Kaylin. "If you want a thing done right," he hissed, whirling his staff over to Vexx. "You have to do it yourself!"

A blast of frost streaked towards him, but Vexx fired a burst of flames, burning it away into nothingness. "I've always felt the same way," he snarled back, rushing forward. He blocked frost bolt after frost bolt, rushing closer as the sounds of the shifting melee echoed around him. Vexx lunged forward, his right hand extended— directly at the rip Kaylin's arrow had torn into the robe.

Vexx fired a burst of flames directly into the ripped part of the robe, the magic fading away as it hit the robe, but sizzling as it burned Barnabus's exposed shoulder. His face twisted in pain as he howled, staggering back. Vexx leaped forward, his left hand extended toward Barnabus's face and fired a powerful bout of flames. The mage crumpled to the ground, dead, and the spirits of the Lowrie Boys nearby died along with him.

Almost at the same instant, the half-dozen surviving guards turned tail and fled, sprinting down the road to Cloudbury. Brundisio hollered in delight as they earned themselves a moment of respite, and Vexx felt him clap him heartily on the shoulder.

"I've never seen fighting like that! I can't believe you killed one of the Lowrie brothers! You shouted your name, too!" The orc berserker chuckled. "You're quite the dungeoneer, Vexx, I'm glad we hired you. I think his brother will be after you though."

Vexx wiped his forehead. "Oh. Great."

"Hey, Vexx?" Kaylin asked, an arrow nocked to her bow, intently studying the nearby forest. "There's still plenty of goblins around, but they're keeping their distance. We really need to get going."

"Oh, right," he muttered, kneeling over beside the frozen wheel, already thawing and dripping into the dirt road. He summoned a brief burst of flames, melting away the ice that coated the wagon wheel. "It's free," he said. "Wait a minute, though. Let's loot the bodies."

"Good thinking, Vexx," Kaylin said as she hopped down. "There might be some good mage stuff on that weirdo!"

"Let's hope so."

"Ooh, this one's only wounded," Shyola said a few paces away, as a man screamed in pain. It was suddenly cut short with a sickening, slurping sound. "Mmm, not bad! These Lowrie Boys have a good flavor to them!"

"Well, I don't think we've seen the end to them," Brundisio muttered. "It's still an hour or two to Cloudbury, and they know we're here. Are you ready for another fight?"

Vexx grinned, pulling out a satchel filled to the brim with magic potions from Barnabus's corpse. "I am now!"

48

GUARDING THE WAGON

The wagon trundled onward through the night, an unearthly sensation as the howls and grunts of the goblins harried them on both sides. Still, aside from the stray arrow fired by reckless goblins and Kaylin, there was little activity. Even after the fighting and despite the late hour, Vexx walked with a spring in his step.

"So, we'll get a bonus for all this lumber?"

"I'll say," Brundisio replied and readied his axes as his eyes swept the perimeter. "We had quite the victory tonight…or we will, once we make it back to Don Kordo's. Never you fear, Vexx White, we'll cut our way through. I've never seen a killer like you."

"Glad to hear it," he said idly, though he felt a certain joy at the prospect. *I'm starting to make a name for myself. Is this what Dred Wyrm felt when he was just starting out?* "You know, you wouldn't be a bad dungeoneer yourself."

"Ah, I'm Don Kordo's right hand orc, and I'm happy staying that way. With the money and reputation we'll win tonight, that's going to mean a lot in the slums." He paused. "I underestimated your companions as well. That she demon...I wouldn't want to tangle with her." He bared his fangs in a smile. "Or maybe I would, if you know what I'm saying."

"I know what you're saying."

"And the elf?" He nodded up at the wagon where Kaylin kept one hand on the reins, the other on her readied bow, eyes scanning for threats. "Normally they're a flighty and weak species, but she can really hold her own."

Kaylin's ear twitched and she looked over. "Thank you," she said, with more than a hint of sarcasm.

"Oh, no problem!" Brundisio called up, then winked at Vexx. "I forgot their hearing is so good," he whispered.

"Eyesight too," Vexx added, "though I suppose you orcs are good in low light. There's no one creeping around?"

Brundisio shrugged. "Just a pack of goblins." He spat to the side. "They're shitting themselves. Goblins are cowards at the best of times, but excellent opportunists. If they see a chance to take us out, they'll charge in an instant. But personally, between you and me?" He shrugged nonchalantly. "They don't have the stones to do it. They'll probably just—"

"Goblins!" Kaylin shouted, pulling on the reins and getting to her feet, drawing her bow back. Vexx saw them now, a great swarm coming in from the side, howling their unearthly chants as they brandished crude scimitars and axes. Vexx's arms shot up and he blasted the front rank with fireballs, a few of the fireballs streaking by overhead to smolder in the branches of nearby pine trees. It cast a dim orange glow on the assault, along with a sickeningly sweet smell from the burning sap.

Brundisio growled, hurling an axe end over end, then grabbed something from his pocket and jammed it into his mouth. He glanced over at Vexx as he chewed, spittle and chunks of food coming out, a wild expression in his eyes that he hadn't had before.

"Stay back, mage," he growled as he chewed. "Time to see how an orc berserker fights! Hah!"

He threw his second axe forward, then ran into the rushing swarm of goblins, swinging his double-headed axe in a long arc that felled the three nearest to him. He moved faster than before, much faster, a whirring blur of gray metal and streaming red blood. Brundisio was howling now, louder than the goblins, as he hacked and slashed away at their bodies. Vexx paused his fireballs as he sat there in awe, watching as a goblin was thwacked clear against the nearest tree, another one hurtling to the ground from the berserker's wild lunge.

The goblins were now running in a panic, but Brundisio kept charging forward. He was faster than them, slashing at their legs, chopping into their backs and downing them, running in close and finishing them off without mercy. When the final goblin fell, he stood there panting.

Shyola whistled, keeping close to the wagon. "You're a bloodthirsty one, orc! I can think of a few hells that would love to have you."

Brundisio made no reply, instead stamping down on a goblin corpse, huffing in exhaustion. The dungeoneers exchanged looks.

"Vexx, can you make him snap out of it?" Kaylin asked. "We need to go."

"Sure thing," Vexx said, walking over to the orc. "Hey Brundisio, nice going! I think that one's dead!"

The orc berserker head whipped around to face him, his wild eyes fixed on Vexx, who stopped. "Uh...hey, buddy." He raised one hand, readying a burst of magic. "You don't want to…"

Brundisio took one heavy step forward, then another. And then the wild look in his eyes faded away, and he shook his head, bits of spittle and phlegm flying into the air.

"Oh, sorry about that, partner!" he said, suddenly calmer. "I get a bit crazy and axe-happy when I take this stuff. I didn't cut you up any, did I?" he asked, glancing up and down at Vexx's robe. "No? You look alright."

"No, it's fine," he said, lowering his hands. "You weren't kidding, though. I think you killed at least a dozen goblins just now."

Brundisio grinned. "What a night, huh? On to Cloudbury and profits!"

Vexx nodded, turning around and waving for Kaylin to continue. They fell in along with the wagon, the night around Cloudbury was silent now, save for the call of an owl. Vexx's breathing slowed to his regular speed, the excitement wearing away, but he still felt energized. The soft creak of leather sounded on the wagon as Kaylin raised herself in the seat.

"What is it?" Vexx asked as the moment lengthened.

Kaylin sighed. "There's a blockade up ahead," she said. "Humans mostly, a few orcs, even an elf."

"The Lowrie Boys," Brundisio intoned, suddenly serious. "Ah, I knew they wouldn't let us just get away this easy."

"Easy?" Vexx snorted. "What about this is easy?"

"Well…" the orc chuckled after a moment. "I guess you're right, mage. Just keep the fire flowing. We'll make it back home in one piece. But *they* won't."

49

BREAKING THE BLOCKADE

The blockade was visible up ahead, a wagon blocking the road along with a few felled trees, crossbowmen sheltering behind the blockade as lanterns lit the surroundings.

"You there!" came a booming voice from the blockade, as Kaylin slowed the wagon to a halt. "Don Kordo's dogs! Who was it that killed my brother?"

A tall mage stood atop the wagon in the middle of the blockade, radiating a glowing shield that covered the entire road. He pointed a finger at them. "I will have your lives!" he screamed, a rough mixture of rage and grief. "Vexx White! Where are you?"

Vexx grimaced, but stood firm. He glanced over at Brundisio. "What do you know about this guy?"

"Don Lowrie," the orc said. "He focuses on buffing and shielding his men. That's part of the reason why their gang is so big. He keeps them alive, and they love him for it."

"Don Lowrie," Vexx muttered, squinting into the

distance. This mage also bore a staff, and Vexx winced as he saw the rippling energy that surged violently through it.

"You humans sure love the name Don," Kaylin commented, carefully selecting her arrows. Brundisio tilted his head up at her, unsure if she was serious.

"They're gang leaders," he said finally. "Vexx, are you ready? There's not much we can do to put this off."

Vexx grunted. "Kaylin, what do you think about creeping off in the woods and taking them out from a distance?"

"Oh?" Kaylin lowered her bow and smiled. "Because of how sneaky I am?"

Shyola snorted. "You're not—"

"Yes, that's exactly why," Vexx cut in. "Sneak around and take a few of them out."

The elf nodded, sliding off the side of the wagon and disappearing into the woods.

"Come on out, or we'll come for you!" Don Lowrie boomed out. "Crossbows, fire a volley!"

Vexx swore and darted towards the wagon as a poorly aimed volley of crossbow bolts soared into the night. There were a few muffled thumps as they sunk into the wagon, others clattered uselessly along the road. The horse whinnied in panic, though Vexx was relieved to see that it was unharmed.

"Damn it. Alright, let's do it," he said. "Straight at them, no fussing about. Leave the wizard to me."

"I'll try," Brundisio said, already chewing on his hallucinogenic mushrooms. "But when the axes start flying, there's no telling what I'll hit." He shot Vexx a wild smile, then bounded down the road.

"Be careful, Master," Shyola said, and then she and Vexx ran toward the blockade. Vexx's heart pounded in his chest as he fired the first fireball straight at Don Lowrie. The fireball hit, but it barely staggered him back, fading away in strength as it passed through the shielding spell.

"Over there!" Don Lowrie shrieked, and several crossbowmen raised themselves out of cover to aim. One of them reeled back, Kaylin's arrow taking him through the ear, but the others fired bolts that just missed the charging dungeoneers, one taking Brundisio in the left ear but not even slowing him down. The orc leaped forward, just as the melee fighters of the Lowrie Boys approached, and Brundisio's surprisingly fast chop bashed a swordsman straight through the helm. The orc slammed down two more times before the others could even react.

One raised a mace in the air, but Shyola's whip slashed forward, cutting it through the haft just as the man struck. He looked over, confused, and Shyola cackled as she leaped forward. The man screamed, trying to resist the succubus as Brundisio tussled with the others. Vexx tossed a fireball into the mix, but kept his focus on the big man atop the wagon, firing up at him even as the mage repelled his attacks. Vexx lowered his attacks, and then concentrated on a powerful Scorching Missile. He shouted as he fired, the Scorching Missile slamming into the wagon, knocking Don Lowrie off balance.

The gang leader cursed as he stumbled back, the spreading flames already enveloping the wagon and setting the boot of a startled crossbowman on fire. The gang member shrieked as the fire began spreading in both directions along the felled trees, and then collapsed to the ground as another arrow soared out from the darkness.

"Onward!" Vexx cried out, blasting the blockade with fireballs as it burst into pieces, kindling flying through the air. Already, a few embers had fallen into the trees nearby, smoldering in the upper branches, and the remaining gang members were backing away warily.

"For my brother!" the mage shouted, raising his staff up high, a burst of wild blue energy crackling out in all directions. The Lowrie Boys, who had been backing up, suddenly straightened. Their faces lost their grim expressions as they suddenly surged forward with a new determined attitude.

Even so, Shyola and Brundisio barreled through them, their flashing whip and double-headed axe felling one and then the other. Vexx kept close behind them, crouching low beside two fresh corpses, pressing his two hands against the bodies. *I've never tried this before. Here goes nothing!*

Sweat beaded his forehead as he forced the necromantic energies downward. His magic reserves were running dangerously low and he slumped onto the ground from the effort. Vexx stared at the defensive circle of Lowrie Boys, one of them stabbing Brundisio in the arm and dodging a swing. Another raised a steel shield, catching Shyola's whip on the edge and shrugging it off, dashing forward with a mace and just missing the succubus as she darted away. She had stopped laughing by now, but darted to the side whilst shooting a worried glance back at Vexx.

Then, his two fresh corpses rose shakily to their feet. Vexx pointed at Don Lowrie. "Kill him," he rumbled, and his undead soldiers lumbered forward. Vexx fired an explosive fireball to clear their paths, and they lurched straight through the collapsing ring of Lowrie Boys, even as Don Lowrie desperately tried to fend them off.

"Tomas, Darrow! Don't...it, it's me!"

The two undead creatures raised their weapons,

smashing the mage's staff aside, then began stabbing away at their former gang leader. As he screamed in pain, the blue energy dissipated around the others, and their ranks broke when they saw their fallen leader. Brundisio slashed one down even as he turned to run, then glanced toward the nearest ones left before darting over to the undead soldiers. Vexx watched as the orc berserker slashed the undead soldiers apart, knocking them to the ground. He winced as the orc's axes slammed into their bodies as they continued to twitch.

Oh well, they served their purpose, Vexx thought, waving Shyola back. He watched Brundisio for a moment. The change seemed to happen in mid-stroke, a sudden shiver as the bloody axe fell, then collapsed onto one of the bodies. It stayed there for a moment, the orc blinking as if surprised to see it there, and then he looked up at Vexx.

"Did we win?" he asked in the sudden silence, sounding almost childlike in his confused innocence, despite the blood soaking his body.

Vexx smiled. "We won."

50

DON KORDO DOES THEM A FAVOR

Vexx couldn't quite remember the rest of the night—how they'd made it past Cloudbury's Western Gate, how they'd escorted it through the slums to Don Kordo, how it came to be emptied of lumber. He knew he'd collapsed into a borrowed bed to sleep like the dead. And then, like many of the dead around him, he'd been forced to rise once again. Vexx rubbed the sleep from his eyes and barely resisted a yawn.

"You what?"

"I have another job for you," Don Kordo said with a smile, looking fresher than ever. "You did so well last night that I saw no reason to wait."

"Did you?" Vexx gave in to a long yawn. "Do you have our money?"

Don Kordo slapped the table, and the large collection of silver coins that rattled on top of it was enough to dash Vexx's exhaustion away. He blinked at the pile.

"Oh! Well, why didn't you say so!"

"And there's more," Don Kordo added, clapping his

hands together. "Have you ever heard of Baron Hardringa?"

"Ah…"

Foggy mentions of the disgraced baron danced through Vexx's memory. Even ensconced in the secluded existence of the Magical Academy at Fallanden, tales of Baron Hardringa had been whispered amongst the students. As a native of Cloudbury, Vexx, of course, remembered them.

"He was a traitor, wasn't he? I don't remember the details exactly."

"The baron would contend that he was not…but it's all the same to me," Don Kordo said with a shrug. "In the end, he wasn't executed, but his title lost all respect. Still, after everything he did, his estate fell into ruins. Over the years, he managed to claim possession of it once again, but it's quite dangerous now. The skeletons of his butchered servants haunt the halls, or so the rumors say. He'd asked me to clear it, but the price was insultingly low, however…" he shrugged. "You dungeoneers seem capable, and the baron did offer what loot could be carried out. So I agreed for you."

"For us," Vexx repeated in disbelief. "Let me guess, for a share of the profits."

Don Kordo shrugged his massive shoulders. "A share of the tiny profits, as it does not include any loot. I'm telling you, I did you a favor. A token of my appreciation after the good work you did me. If you hadn't fallen in with me, you would never even have heard about this quest."

"I suppose not," Vexx said, scooping his reward into his coin purse. "And this renegade baron? Where can he be found?"

"There's a detached servant's cottage outside his haunted halls where he's been staying. You know nobles, there's nothing as demeaning as living like the common folk. He doesn't have much money, but he still has his pride." Don Kordo pointed out the window. "It's just outside the wall and still flies his family crest. You can't miss it."

Vexx nodded. "I'll go wake the others," he said, and turned to make his way through the creaking house. He hesitated at one of the guest doors for a moment, then rapped sharply on the aged wood. "Kaylin! Got another job!"

A groan echoed from within. "Can I just have a few minutes?"

"Time is money," he said. "Get on up!" Vexx stepped over to the next door. *I sound like my father*, he thought to himself. *Or like one of the damned instructors.* Before he could knock on the door, it swung open. Shyola flashed him a coy smile and looked as energetic as ever.

"Why, Master! Coming to my private quarters, I see."

"We've got another job. Ready for it?"

"Absolutely. I couldn't sleep at all last night. I was so worked up after draining those lovely souls. I need to work out this energy somehow," she said, biting her lip seductively. "Who are we killing next?"

"They're undead," Vexx replied. "No souls here."

"Ah, that should be fine. Just as long as they're not goblins. I've had more than enough of those filthy creatures."

"You and me both," Vexx muttered as Kaylin's door creaked open. She shuffled out, bleary-eyed and yawning.

"Where are we going?"

"To make our fortunes," Vexx declared, striding through the house like a conquering hero. "After me!"

❦

THE SERVANT'S cottage was a far cry from the slums of Western Cloudbury, but the man who answered their knocks seemed to be only a shell of his former self.

"Baron Hardringa, I presume," Vexx said at the doorway.

"Yes. Normally, I would have my butler answer, but he is, ahem, undead. As are most of my family. You must have heard the details."

"Not exactly," Vexx replied, "but never mind that. We'll put him down for good."

The baron smiled wanly. "It warms my heart to hear that. You must be some of Don Kordo's mercenaries. He sent word that he'd send someone to solve my little problem."

"Ah. Dungeoneers would be the term, my lord. We raid for ancient loot and solve problems for the townsfolk."

"Indeed?" Baron Hardringa's eyebrows rose. "Well, I suppose I am just a simple city dweller by now, and my home has fallen into ruins. Help me, brave dungeoneers, and I will be forever in your debt."

Vexx cracked his knuckles and flashed a cocky smile. "Never you fear, Baron. Vexx White is on the quest!"

51

CLEARING THE HARDRINGA ESTATE

The first skeletons emerged before they had even passed the ruined gardens, a surprisingly quick spear thrust took Vexx by surprise. He swore and dodged aside, then slammed the reanimated skeleton with a fireball.

"Where the hell did he come from?"

"Perhaps he was a gardener," Shyola replied, slashing through the overgrown hedges with her whip. It provided a better view of the ruined exterior of the Hardringa Estate. An ornate marble fountain had partially collapsed in an outside plaza, which was further marred by bird droppings and vegetation in various stages of rot. Vines scaled their way up the walls of the manor building, a shed by the side had been left unattended, and the beginnings of a small tree emerged from the cracked tiles of the nearby plaza. It must have been impressive, once. But that time had passed years ago.

"I wish we could just burn the place down," Vexx grumbled.

"You just want to burn everything down," Kaylin pointed out.

"It does make things easier." Vexx sighed. "Let's go through the ground entrance there," he said, jerking his chin at the rotting door nearest to them. It had been painted a garish yellow, but it had faded away from the constant battering of sunlight and now sported what looked like deep gouges from wild animals. "We'll work our way to the top," he added, heaving an internal sigh as he looked up at the three stories of the ruined manor. "That goes up pretty high."

Kaylin snorted. "No, it does not. By human standards, maybe, but in an Elven tree village, you could be many spans higher. Up in the clouds, practically. This is nothing."

"For once, I agree with the elf," Shyola said. "You should have seen the spires of the Old Empire, Master. They circled their way into the sky—but that was before the devastation that came afterward. That I..." she paused. "Ah...I shall save those stories for another time."

"Huh, are you saying that you're the reason the Old Empire fell?" Vexx laughed at the thought, but Shyola's expression was unusually serious.

"It has been said of me," she said diplomatically. "But never mind that. Let's destroy some skeletons in the ruins of a ruined Empire."

Vexx tilted his head, unsure how to process this new information, but finally nodded. "Shyola, why don't you go first? We'll cover you from behind."

"Certainly, Master," Shyola said, sauntering towards the door. "You can cover my behind." She sped up as she neared the door, slamming into it with her shoulder, and strode into the ruined manor. "Oh, skeletons! Damned souls!" She snapped her whip into existence. "Come out and get me!"

"Well, that's one approach," Vexx muttered as he and Kaylin squeezed in after her, hearing rumbles and hisses from every direction. The gleam of white caught his eye, and he cursed as a pair of reanimated skeletons shuffled forward, cudgels in their hands. Shyola slashed forward in a flash, severing them both in half. She stepped forward into the open, a few spiraling staircases visible on both sides, and spun around with a feral smile fixed to her face.

"Come out and play!"

From the upper floor, a shambling horde of skeletons approached in both directions. Vexx turned to face the left side and downed one with a quick fireball. "Kaylin, guard the right," he snapped, noticing that she'd kept her bow strapped to her back. The elf was swinging around one of her net traps, but this one was weighted down with a dozen stones. "What are you doing?"

"Arrows are useless against those things," she replied, swinging the net around. "Trust me, I've got this!" Kaylin flung the net up into the staircase, catching a few skeletons inside it, and with a shout that echoed throughout the room, she yanked back. The skeletons fell tumbling to the ground floor, their fragile bones shattering from the impact. Kaylin grinned as she began swinging her net again. "This thing works great!"

A few other skeletons had emerged from rooms in the ground floor, and Shyola darted forward to meet them, but Vexx focused his attention back on the staircase to his left. He carefully fired fireball after fireball, making each shot count this time, taking skeletons full in the chest and smashing them to pieces. With a roar, he quickened his pace, downing a half-dozen in just a few seconds, then paused to drink one of his magic potions. With the haul from Barnabus Lowrie, Vexx saw little reason to ration them, and he belched as the potion worked its way into his body.

A bit of spearmint would help the flavor, he thought, recalling Doctor Fansee. *But it's the boost in stamina it gives me that really helps.*

Vexx's hands shot forward, his fireballs knocking down another half-dozen advancing skeletons. Shy's whip cracked, and he heard Kaylin's grunting, followed by the smashing of bones on the ground. Already, the advancing skeletons thinned down to no more than twenty, and with each one smashed to bits, they dwindled further and further in ranks.

Easy money, Vexx thought, just as Kaylin screamed.

Vexx knocked a few of the last skeletons back before turning in alarm. "What is it?" he asked, then saw a flash of black and red.

"A hellbeast!" Shyola cried out, turning to face the right staircase, a pile of smashed bones littering the ground around her. It was tangled in Kaylin's net, but the hellbeast roared, an unearthly howl that shook the very foundations of the manor. The net began to smolder and burn. Vexx turned and fired, watching as his fireballs slammed into the hellbeast. It leaped through the air and Kaylin sprinted aside, her frantic fingers fumbling at the strap of leather holding her bow in place. Shyola's whip cracked just above the hellbeast as it ducked low to avoid her attacks.

The creature leaped up in the air at Shyola, one huge paw slamming her to the ground as she tried to dodge away, shattering the tile floor below her. The beast roared its demonic howl again as it pinned her down. An arrow sunk deep into its flank just as Vexx ran over, switching to frost magic, and he fired a burst of frost into its mouth just as it went for Shyola's neck. The succubus screamed in fright, but the ravenous jaws of the hellbeast froze into place. A moment later, the ice began to crackle.

I hate frost magic, Vexx thought, rushing close. But how else do I kill that thing?

Another arrow took it in the jaw and a whimper echoed over the snapping of the ice. And when Shy wriggled herself free, she slashed her whip upward. Against its thick, scaly armor, the whip didn't appear to do a thing—but she slashed again and again, even as the frost cracked away. Vexx stuck both arms forward, feeding more magic into the ice, keeping the hellbeast stuck fast. Then Shyola slashed again, tearing it clean through the heart, and the hellbeast slumped to the ground.

Vexx let out a long sigh as Shyola slithered free from under the beast's corpse.

"Vexx, behind you!" Kaylin snapped, and in an instant, he turned around, magic readied.

A walking corpse confronted him. *Or...not quite.* Vexx blinked and took a second to take in the aged and gaunt appearance of Baron Hardringa. The old aristocrat frowned as he looked around.

"This is not as it used to be," he muttered.

"We're working here," Vexx snapped, glancing around. "Come back later."

"I think we've got them all, darling," Shyola said, flicking a spot of dried blood off her skin. "Though I did not expect a hellbeast in this realm."

"Oh yes, my dear old foxhound," Baron Hardringa said sadly. "So that's what happened to you, you poor old thing."

Vexx grunted. "We're off, then. I trust you've paid Don Kordo."

"Every last penny." The baron paused. "Well, you're going to help me clean this up, aren't you?"

Vexx laughed as he turned to walk up the dilapidated stairs. "We'll take a few things, but that's it."

The baron grunted. "Common folk. I will never understand you lot."

52

AGREEING TO DISAGREE

"I put three arrows into that hellbeast," Kaylin insisted as they walked through the streets of Cloudbury, liberated coins and trinkets jangling as they went along. "Not to mention, I was the one who trapped it in the first place."

"Vexx trapped it," Shyola replied, "my cunning Master saving my life with such skillful frost magic! Oh, I won out in the end, cutting my way free and felling the beast. But I can't take credit alone."

"I just don't know why you keep saying I'm useless," Kaylin said darkly, frowning over at the succubus. "I do plenty of things to help us! To help you, even! Tell her, Vexx."

"I didn't say you're useless, elf, I said that you're baggage. I imagine we could get some coin for you."

"Knock it off, Shy," Vexx said, finally losing his patience. "You make a good team, despite it all, so stop pretending that you don't."

The succubus sniffed, but said nothing further. Kaylin

stuck her head out, blinking. "Hey, Vexx! There's something on the board by the inn. Want to check it out?"

"Really?" Vexx perked up. Ever since they had returned to Cloudbury, he'd never seen any bounties posted, or at least nothing he was authorized to carry out. Vexx hurried over, the other dungeoneers right behind, and they crowded around the bounty that still smelled of fresh glue. "The Church posted this," Vexx said, skimming through it. "Stolen goods? Last night?"

"This is horrible!" Shyola declared, and Kaylin and Vexx both looked over in surprise. "What? It really is horrible! The bounty is posted out here, available to anyone! Let's tear it off, Master, so no one else gets a chance to get the reward."

"Tear it off?" Kaylin sputtered. "Why, that's...that's..." she blinked. "An incredibly good idea," she said as she quickly grabbed the paper and ripped it off the board. She rolled it up and handed it over to Vexx. "Good thinking," she added.

Shyola smiled uncertainly. "Ah...thank you."

"It's a bit light on details," Vexx said, glancing over the bounty in his hands. "But apparently, a group of thieves stole the golden artifacts from the reliquary last night. The Church wants them back and is offering quite a lot for it. Oh, this is great!" He rolled it up and favored the other two dungeoneers with a wide smile before sticking the paper in his robes. "Things are going really well for us lately! We do this job and we might as well call ourselves the next Dred Wyrms!"

"That's a terrible name, Master, and I won't be calling myself that anytime soon. That said, we should do this quest at once."

"I agree," Kaylin added happily. "With both of those things."

Shyola shifted her feet. "Stop agreeing with me," she muttered. "It's weird."

"It is a little weird," Kaylin agreed again. "But when you're right, you're right."

"Let's go to Don Kordo first," Vexx said, lost in thought. "Someone might have sold it to them. Then, we can ask around at the reliquary. I'm sure they have a few clues."

The dungeoneers rushed through the traffic to make their way back to Don Kordo. Brundisio greeted them at the door, a fresh bandage on his torn ear. "Ah, the brave dungeoneers have returned! I heard you cleared out Baron Hardringa's manor just this morning. Will your adventures ever end?"

"No," Vexx said, pushing his way past and slowly opening the door, feeling the tingle of the magical enchantment. Don Kordo looked up from his desk in surprise.

"Back so soon? I just gave you the baron's reward not an hour ago!"

Vexx unrolled the bounty poster, tapping the scroll. "Golden artifacts from the reliquary were stolen last night. Do you know anything about that?"

"What? No. I mean, I'd be interested if the price was right. But I've been plenty busy sorting out this Lowrie Gang business."

"Hmmm..." Vexx nodded. "Well, if you hear anything, let me know."

"What are you doing with that bounty poster?" Don Kordo asked in puzzlement.

"Oh, we just tore it off."

"You're not supposed to do that," Don Kordo sputtered. "What if someone else wants the job?"

Vexx sighed. "You've been very helpful," he said, turning to leave. "Come on, off to the reliquary."

53

HELPING THE CHURCH

"This is…" the stern, hawk-nosed countenance of Gaius flickered between confusion and outrage. The tall priest just shook his head after a moment. "Most…irregular."

"What's irregular?" Vexx asked, radiating innocence, spreading his arms wide.

"Your family name isn't exactly held in renown, White boy. And this elf here—"

"Why does everyone keep calling me that…" Vexx muttered.

"She should not be in the presence of a holy site. But even worse…" Gaius shook his head in disbelief. "Does that harlot have blood on her bosom?"

"Yes…" Shyola purred. "Would you like to lick—"

"On second thought," Vexx snapped, raising a hand in front of Shyola. "You do have a point. But look here!" he said, producing a loose sheaf of paper. "We saw your bounty posted and ripped it down. It says some of your gold artifacts were stolen just last night. We can handle—"

"You what!? That was for bounty hunters to pursue!"

"Right…but what I'm saying is that we're bounty hunters. Anyway, it says some gold artifacts were stolen from the church and—"

Gaius's hand whipped forward and snatched the poster away from Vexx.

"Hey!"

"I've had just about enough of you," he huffed. "Why, you—"

"One moment, sir," Vexx said, brandishing his scrolls. "Are you still in the market for literature and curios?"

The priest hesitated a moment, emotions warring on his face. His glare fell a fraction. "Perhaps."

"Check this out," Vexx said, unfolding a scene of erotic dryad art. "What a lucky satyr he is, with all the dryads—"

"Leave this place and never come here again!" Gaius shouted as he quickly ushered them out and slammed the door behind them.

"Okay, we'll come by later!" Vexx sniffed, glancing at his two companions. "That could have gone better."

"I thought you did wonderfully, darling," Shyola said as she patted his arm. "Only, perhaps we could kill them next time? That strapping young priest had the most wonderful smell of innocence about him."

"I became a dungeoneer to kill monsters," Kaylin said in a small voice, shaking her head in sadness. "Have I become a monster myself?" She raised her hands in the air. "What evil have these hands caused in freeing you from your cage?"

"Oh come now, dear, those hands are not evil hands," Shyola said, in a tone that sounded strangely like genuine kindness. It was ruined a moment later. "But they do look delicious. Could I just have a nibble—"

Kaylin jerked her hands away. "No."

Shy bit her lip. "Perhaps I've been too harsh to my Master's helpful assistant. It was the hunger, I suspect. You're not yourself when you're hungry."

"That's true," Kaylin said with a nod. "But I'm no assistant, and I've never been helpful to anyone. Just ask Vexx."

"That's true. We're partners," Vexx added.

Shy scowled. "No, I don't like that. I don't like that one bit." She sighed. "Where to next, Master? It seems this is a dead end."

"Hmm…" Vexx pursed his lips. "I suspect the barkeep may have found out about his dead sheep by now…and I doubt he's forgiven us for breaking his chair. Though it was the dwarf's doing."

"Strange what you two were up to before I came along," Shy said thoughtfully. "Though in my experience, it's always best to blame a dwarf. Hang on, though, something has occurred to me. These priests, they don't actually need to *agree*, do they?"

Vexx frowned. "I realize you're a succubus, but consent is important."

"No, what I mean is, we can just find the artifacts and return them. For a hefty reward! Oh, you think their Supreme Leader will let me take the priest as a reward?"

Kaylin and Vexx exchanged skeptical glances.

"You know, Vexx, she has a point about the artifacts. *If* we can track down whoever did this."

"Right. They don't have Supreme Leaders, though. I think you're thinking of death cults," Vexx pointed out.

"Ah…well, I have much more experience with them than with these church types. You see that bakery just across the way?" Shy pointed across the street. "Bakers begin their mornings very early. They're great for a midnight snack! The, uh…bread, I mean. Anyway, perhaps one of them saw something."

Vexx whistled. "Well, now! It'll be great not being the only one coming up with ideas! Let's go."

Kaylin grinned over at Shy. "Vexx has always been good at ideas."

54

THE BAKERY

The powdery-whiskered gnome in charge of the bakery nodded once as Vexx made his request clear. "Sure, Maug and Linda were here overnight. They might have seen something; they're farrenweed smokers and take pretty regular breaks. Great workers, though," the gnome mused.

"Great, so we can have a chat with them?"

The shrewd baker raised a hand to stop Vexx. "That's taking time away from work for my two best employees, you know! They love kneading dough and hate stopping. Well, unless it's to smoke farrenweed, but they would feel terrible if..."

He trailed off as a couple coppers hit the table in front of him.

"They'd still feel a bit bad, you know, they love their work so much that—"

A few more coppers pinged onto the table. After a long moment, Vexx sighed and placed a fifth down firmly.

"I can work with that. I take my employees' well being seriously, you know," the gnome said, scooping up the coins with a wide grin. "Maug! Linda!" he shouted, banging on the solid door behind him. He nodded back at the others. "They'll be right out. Don't keep them more than a few minutes, alright? I've got loaves that need kneading. Speaking of which, can I interest you in anything?"

"I'll pick up some supplies, Vexx," Kaylin said, glancing over at Shyola. "Just for the two of us, though."

The succubus scoffed. "Suit yourself. I'll stick to meat. Fresh, wriggling, screaming meat."

The door slammed open before Kaylin could respond, and everyone looked up at the new arrival. Or arrivals. A two-headed ogre stood before them, one head brushing the ceiling, a woman's face with intricately braided purple hair looking down at them.

"Yes, boss?" she asked. The other head lolled to the side, a male face daubed with red and white warpaint looked back at them. "Yeth bawth?" it asked, slurring its words.

"Maug, Linda, these fine people have some questions for you. It seems there was a bit of a whoopsie-daisy at the reliquary across the street and the fine folks of the church lost a few items. These dungeoneers would like to know if you noticed anything. You'd have been working here at the time."

"Ohhh…" Linda said, the arm nearest to her face stroking her chin as if she was lost in thought. "That would make sense. I did see a group leaving the reliquary in the middle of the night."

"Wath relkwary?" Maug asked, blinking, the other arm scratching at his patchy head in confusion.

"I think I'll just talk with Linda, thank you very much Maug," Vexx said politely to the towering two-headed ogre. "How many of them would you say there were? And what direction were they headed in?"

The ogre instantly pointed both left and right. The two heads swivelled to look at each other and a heated series of whispers ensued. Finally, the male head nodded, his face flushed with his slight embarrassment, and he pointed in the same direction as the left arm. Linda nodded in satisfaction, her massive curls of purple hair teetering precariously in the air.

"Oh, six or so, which I did think was unusual," she said. "And they were hauling things out of the reliquary. When they reached the intersection, they hurried straight down Tower Road. Ah, so that would that be…"

"Noth."

"Oh yes, thanks Maug. Yes, they definitely headed North. They didn't seem to turn on any other streets, though truth be told, I wasn't watching too closely."

"Yaugh, we wath thmokin'," Maug grunted out. Linda nodded beside him, and the two-headed ogre clapped its hands together, sending a small burst of powder into the air.

"Alright, best get back to it," the gnome said after a moment, once it was clear Vexx had no further questions. "Those bagels won't curl themselves."

"Oh! One thing!" The massive ogre paused, Maug looking back. "Gobs."

Vexx blinked. "What?"

"Gob'ns."

After a moment, the ogre turned again, Linda craning her head over. "He means they were goblins, and now that I think about it, Maug is right. You people all look little to me, but they were littler than most. Like the boss here," Linda added, pointing down to the gnome.

He sniffed. "I look nothing like a goblin. Back to it, you two."

The floor rocked as Maug and Linda pushed open the interior door behind them, and the three dungeoneers made their way outside, the bell on the entrance ringing as the door closed behind them.

"Five coppers," Shyola muttered as they came to a stop just outside. "We can't go spending money like that, Master. I could have simply possessed that ogre and dragged out our answers that way."

"Which one?" Vexx asked.

Shy frowned. "I'm not exactly sure how that would have worked."

"Anyway, five copper coins is nothing. Do you remember the reward? 100 gold coins. We could be rich after this!"

Shyola nodded slowly. "I've been trapped in a book for centuries and most unearthly realms don't make much use of non-soul-based currency. 100 gold coins is...good?"

Vexx's jaw fell open. "Is it...good? Is...is 100 gold coins..." he looked over to Kaylin helplessly. "I mean, you tell her Kaylin. That's a lot!"

Kaylin's expression looked even blanker than usual. "Yeah...I'm really not sure how much that's worth. How much bread does that get you?"

Vexx sighed. "At least you two finally have something in common. Okay, look. We've been scraping by with coppers and the odd silver, but gold? Gold is on a whole 'nother level. We could buy a *mount* for that much, if we really wanted to."

"Mmm, that does sound good," Shyola said to herself.

Vexx shook his head in frustration. "Look, just leave the business of money to me. The church really wants their stuff back, and this reward proves that, if nothing else. I snatched the poster, but I'm sure word has gone around. There could be clerics and paladins poking around here before too long, or some high-level dungeoneers. But we're the first ones here and we have a solid lead. Let's track these thieving bastards down before we get competition."

Shy nodded. "Got it. If paladins show up, I *will* drain their souls, Master. That isn't negotiable, bond or not."

"I can work with that," Vexx muttered, then stuck his hand out between them. "Are you with me?"

Kaylin put her hand in. "I'm with you!"

Shy followed a moment later. "I don't like how she's touching you, Master," she grumbled. "But I can work with the elf on this."

"Good," Vexx said, smiling as they released their hands. *It feels like we're finally a team. Nothing can stand in our way!*

"We could use the extra bread money," Kaylin said dubiously, "but Vexx, I don't think I want to eat a mount."

He sighed. "That's fine, Kaylin. Alright, let's head down Tower Road."

55

HEADING DOWN TOWER ROAD

Kaylin slowed partway through the street and pointed to the left. "Hey, it's that tavern! We usually see it from the other end, but there are some windows facing outward to Tower Road. Someone might have seen something."

Vexx grimaced as he took in the barred windows. "I don't know...I mean, we kind of killed his sheep," he said, glancing over at Shyola.

"Oh, that's him?" Shy chuckled. "I wonder if he's noticed—"

Kaylin had already opened the door, calling out a cheery hello to the barkeep, and Vexx kept his sinking feelings to himself as he slunk in behind her. A few heads turned his way, skipping past him and locking onto Shyola, but the tavern was mostly empty. Vexx slowly trudged up to where Kaylin was trying to attract the attention of the stone-faced barkeep.

He looked over at Vexx and frowned. "You! You've got a lot of nerve coming back here. First of all, goblins are still stealing my sheep. Second, you and that dwarf broke one of my chairs with your stupid antics!"

"What? You can't put that on us," Vexx sputtered, trying not to look too guilty. "We killed the goblin you told us to, and anyway, it was the dwarf that broke the chair. You know how they get."

Pollander scowled. "I will not tolerate racist comments in my establishment!"

"I'm just saying! We were all thinking it!" He nudged Kaylin, who looked distinctly uncomfortable. "Right? Well, anyway, we can make things right."

"Huh, how's that?" the barkeep scoffed. "I'm not paying you again."

"No, no, we'll do this out of the goodness of our hearts," Vexx lied. "We'll trek up to the Lifeless Hills and hunt down the goblins who've been killing your sheep as a gesture of appreciation for you and what you've been through."

"The goodness of your hearts, huh?" the barkeep asked, calm and slow, looking from Kaylin to Vexx to Shyola. Finally, he shrugged and expectedly dabbed at the corner of one eye. "It just feels good to…you know." He paused. "Be appreciated. Alright!" he said in a hearty voice, unsuccessfully hiding his emotions. "If you really do mean that, I'll throw in a round of ale when you come back successfully."

"You got it," Vexx said. "Will goblin ears do?"

"Hmm, normally yes, but…truth be told, I'm not entirely sure it was a goblin this time. The things they did to my poor sheep…you know, my neighbor down the way had strange circles put into his crops. He thinks there might be cultists up in those hills. Necromancers, proba-bly. You can never trust a necromancer."

"That's true."

The barkeep shook his head sadly. "It was a shame what happened to that poor sheep."

"Sounds terrible," Shyola added with a poorly concealed smirk. Vexx tapped her arm and shot her a glare before smiling at the barkeep.

"Oh, as it happens…you wouldn't happen to have heard anything usual? I mean, goblins raiding this far into town or… strange sounds last night? I just want to be thorough about finding justice for your sheep."

"Well, now that you mention it…" Pollander leaned over the counter. "Carl!" he shouted. In the corner, an orc slowly emerged, one eye blackened, his face downcast. A mace hung from his belt, but aside from his leather shorts, he didn't appear to be wearing much.

"Can you…keep it…down. Hung…over."

"Yeah, he's a regular," Pollander said to Vexx. "Now, Carl, can you tell the good people what you told me? About the commotion last night."

"Oh yeah," the orc said with a smile. "We were playing cards and this logger got into a fight with—"

"No, no, not that," the barkeep interrupted. "I mean later, when I was closing up."

"Oh yeah!" Carl burped, reeking like a half-opened casket of ale. "Hmm…s'cuse me. So anyway, I was rooting around for vegetable scraps in the alley, right, when all of a sudden, this band of thieves runs right down Tower Road! Plain as day, 'cept it was late at night."

"Really…did you happen to get a peek at them, Carl?"

"Eh…" he snorted, rubbing his tusk and protruding snout. "Might've. Buy me a drink?"

Vexx shrugged, spreading his arms wide, and looked

over at the barkeep. With the mostly empty bar, the man seemed content to take it easy and watch.

"A drink for the gentleman here."

"Hornswaggle whiskey!" Carl shouted. "Make it a double! Neat!"

The barkeep winced. "You don't need to shout. I thought you were hungover," he muttered, rummaging through his stores. "Oh, and that'll be seven coppers."

"Seven!?" Vexx sputtered.

"It's imported from across the sea," Pollander said, pouring a double measure. "I'm not charging you for that chair, kid. Count your blessings."

Carl grinned as he was handed the drink. "Cheers!"

"Start talking," Vexx said, the moment Carl set it down. "How many were there?"

The orc let out a big belch and fixed his gap-toothed smile on Vexx. "Sure thing, pal. Seven, maybe? Five at least."

Vexx nodded. "Did they appear to be carrying anything?"

"Oh yeah, some big stuff! Shiny too, the moonlight kinda...flickered on them, you know? Oh..." Carl blinked. "That might've been gold. I think it was!"

"Settle down," Vexx said. "What kind of species were they? Any other identifiable features?"

"They wore black. Like a uniform, almost. Ah...I suppose they weren't too big. Coulda been, you know. Dwarves, gnomes, that sort of thing."

"Goblins?" Vexx prompted.

Carl chuckled. "I mean, I guess? Goblins don't come into town. They might raid the outskirts, but..." he shrugged.

"Got it," Vexx said, already leaving. He exchanged

glances with Shy and Kaylin. *At least the witnesses are consistent. But what does it all mean?*

"Oh…they went down Tower Road, you know," Carl said, draining the last of his Hornswaggle whiskey. "Followed it uphill as far as I could see."

Vexx nodded, already turning. Shy and Kaylin stayed silent as they weaved their way through the empty chairs and tables. A few moments later, they stepped outside the tavern and Vexx glanced over to the Lifeless Hills in the distance.

Are the church's relics somewhere up there? I guess there's only one way of finding out.

"We'll have to pick up some potions," Vexx said, already turning to the market. "I'm out—"

He stopped as Shyola grabbed his shoulder. "It's too late for that," she said in a low voice. "Look over there," Shy whispered, and Vexx glanced over.

A boy was plastering glue against the poster board beside the tavern, a fresh poster in his hand, big bold text declaring a bounty posted by the church. The dungeoneers stayed rooted there as the boy slapped the poster, pressing firmly down on the edges, and stood back to admire his work.

A moment later, the boy took off, swinging the tools in hands and whistling as he went down the street. The instant he turned the corner, Vexx snuck forward and snatched the poster off the board. He shredded it a few times, then stuck the remnants of it into his robes.

"We have maybe a few hours, tops, before other dungeoneers begin moving in on our quest," Vexx said. "A haul like this could be our ticket out of this sleepy little town. We've gotta get going, *now!*"

56

ONE STEP AHEAD

"Those are definitely goblin tracks," Kaylin said, staring at the muddy prints leading up the slope from the northern end of Tower Road. "I'm sure of it."

"How can you be sure?" Vexx asked. "I know your eyesight is good, but those tracks could have been made from anything."

"It's not just the tracks. Look there," she said, pointing beside a bush.

Vexx leaned it close. Whatever it was, it didn't smell too good.

"Goblin scat," Kaylin announced. "And still fresh."

Vexx wrinkled his nose. "You could have told me…"

"Yeah, I would sometimes come across scat like that in the woods outside my village," Kaylin said, with more than a little pride in her voice. "That's likely a half-day old. I'd stake my life on it."

"Your life? Mmm, I hope you're wrong," Shyola cut in.

"Either way, let's find out," Vexx said, scanning the tracks as they rose up and away from Cloudbury. "That's a pretty clear path up to the Lifeless Hills. Interesting that they worked their way into town and walked several blocks before looting a place with priceless artifacts."

"What are you saying?" Shyola asked after a moment.

"I'm not saying anything," Vexx said, but a suspicion had already taken hold of him. He thought about it for a few moments but decided to keep it to himself. Shyola would just propose draining the life from potential suspects, and it would take much too long to explain his theory to Kaylin. So he waved them onward and began marching up to the Lifeless Hills. "Let's go!"

❧

VEXX WIPED beads of sweat from his forehead as he struggled to keep moving forward. This was rough country by any measure, especially in the sweltering heat during the day, though darkness came early in this land. For a moment, he stood on a rock outcrop to look out at the setting sun. Win or lose, they'd be camping out here tonight. He wasn't entirely sure how he felt about that.

Shy pushed through the yellowed grass below him, breathing heavily as well. *It's a bit relieving to see that even demons can tire. And this angle provides a great view of her...*

Shyola glanced up, seeming to read his thoughts, and the succubus gave him a coy smile as she raised a hand up to him. "Give me a tug, Master. You know I'd give you a tug if you wanted it."

Vexx reached down and hauled her up beside him. Her fingers trailed lightly over his arm and he tried his best to ignore her antics. She stepped away and glanced over to the next ridge. Below them, Kaylin staggered to the side as she struggled to heave herself over some loose stones and took a precarious step on a patch of grass and mountain flowers.

"Like the demon said," Kaylin said, sticking her hand up towards Vexx. "Give me a tug, and I'll give you a tug."

Shy snorted behind them. "You know, I don't like it quite as much when you say it, elf."

"Why?" she asked in genuine curiosity. Shy didn't bother replying.

Vexx licked his lips, already regretting their departure from Cloudbury. They'd left so hastily, they hadn't even had the chance to refill their water flasks.

I have a little bit of health potion left. Would it be absurd if I used it to stay hydrated? Vexx thought about it a moment. Six goblins at least. *No, I better save it for an emergency.*

"Hey…I think I can make out a cave up here," Kaylin said, breaking into his thoughts. She leaned to the side and brushed aside a few strands of hair that clung to her damp forehead. "Yes, that's definitely a big cave. Want to scout it out?"

"A big one," Shy said sarcastically. "Like the last half-dozen we'd checked?"

Vexx tried to ignore the constant bickering. It was true, though. So far, all the cave entrances they'd found had barely gone anywhere. *The goblins must be hiding in a cave here somewhere, and it must be a huge one to keep all them, their supplies, and the loot from the church. But how did they know how and where to loot it? Something doesn't seem right here…*

"Yes, I know what a big one is," Kaylin snapped in response to one of Shyola's sarcastic questions.

"Do you?" she asked, laying on the sarcasm thick. "Because—"

"Ladies!" Vexx snapped. "Let's not do this, alright? Kaylin, would you mind scouting out the cave while Shy and I rest here."

"Really?" Kaylin blinked her big green eyes at him, and he felt something in his chest loosen. "Why's that, Vexx?"

"Because you're a nimble elf," he replied. "Good at spotting things and you're...graceful."

"Really?" She beamed. "You really think so?"

"I do," Vexx lied and ignored Shy's incredulous snort.

"The other elves always said I was clumsy," Kaylin said, looking up at the cave with a determined set to her jaw. "I'll show them. I'll show them all," she said, and began marching upward.

"Great. Have fun," Vexx called out after her.

"That was good thinking, Vexx," Shy said after a moment. "Have her 'scout' the empty cave. It gives us some time to ourselves. So what position do you want me in?"

"Cover our rear."

"Ooh, that sounds very nau..." Shy trailed off. "Oh, you're serious."

"I'll watch the cave entrance," Vexx said. "To make sure Kaylin doesn't get into any trouble."

Shyola sighed in frustration. "You spend too much time watching her. She'll be fine! Or she'll die. Does it really matter either way?"

Vexx made no response.

Nearing the entrance above, Kaylin slipped and stumbled down a few feet before recovering. After a moment, she got to her feet and looked back. She shot Vexx a thumbs up and a weak smile. Then she ducked into the narrow cave entrance.

And the waiting began.

57

NIGHTFALL IN THE LIFELESS HILLS

Vexx blew into his cupped hands and tried to make himself as small as possible by the large boulder he was hiding behind. He vigorously rubbed his arms as he tried his best to stay warm. The sun had disappeared behind the ridges, casting this part of the Lifeless Hills in shadow, and the temperature had already plummeted.

"I'm wearing so very little," Shy said, though she didn't seem bothered by the weather at all. "Vexx, could we curl up together for warmth?"

"You're fine."

The silence lingered.

"It's Kaylin, isn't it?" Shy asked.

"What?" Vexx asked, still staring at the cave entrance. *It's been too long now.*

Shyola sighed in exasperation. "You know, my last master died of old age. He was so boring! I was hoping a vivacious young man like yourself would make use of me. But…nothing! And after all those centuries."

Vexx grimaced. "I don't know what to say."

"Admit it. You have a thing for her."

"No!" Vexx protested. "She's an elf. And she's stupid, naive, and clumsy, and…and…" he fell silent. "We have to save her."

Shy scoffed. "I know you feel that way, but the thing is…despite her idiocy, she's surprisingly resilient. You don't—"

"No, I mean, look! Up there!"

Vexx pointed up the slope to where two goblins with torches had emerged. They sniffed the area, spreading out to both sides, scanning and grunting to each other. *That can only mean one thing. Kaylin found them! And she's been…*

Vexx couldn't even entertain the thought of her dying. *She's been…captured. We have to save her!*

Silently, Vexx crept forward, Shyola right behind him. Vexx gestured to one of the goblins with an outstretched hand, and Shy crept off in that direction, silent as she chose each step with care. Vexx swallowed as he made for the other one, a thin trail of dirt drifting down the hill with each step, though he kept quiet as he neared the goblin. They didn't appear to be too observant. At the very least, their night vision was completely ruined by the torches they held.

The goblin nearest Vexx grumbled something, likely a complaint about being on sentry duty or something of the sort, but it wasn't like the goblin language that had been on the curriculum at the magical academy. *Neither was knife work,* Vexx thought, hesitating as his hand hovered above the sturdy handle. *How can I kill silently?*

Vexx had always been attracted to the Black Arts, but was an amateur at best, since that sort of magic had been banned from the curriculum. Following that, he'd been decent at fire magic, but he knew a smattering of all sorts. *Besides healing. I never had the knack for that…not that I'll need it for this.*

He glanced over to the left, wincing at the brightness of the second goblin's torch, and could just barely make out the sinuous outline of Shyola as she hunted from the shadows. *That poor goblin bastard. He's about to lose his soul.*

Vexx's eyes snapped back forward to his own target. There was no hesitating now. The fingertips of his right hand chilled as icicles came into existence, a microclimate of frost blossoming around his hand. Vexx stalked forward and held his breath as he inched closer and closer. *I'm no expert with ice magic, but it should do the trick. After all…*

Vexx sprang forward, the cold wind extinguishing the torch in an instant, ice freezing and hardening all around the goblin's face. *You can't scream for help if your head is frozen!*

The goblin collapsed to the ground in the sudden darkness, and Vexx turned just as he heard some small gasp. Shyola was right behind the goblin, her flickering orange whip around him, but she retracted it in an instant. That same flickering orange energy encircled the goblin before mysteriously dissipating. For a moment, Vexx was left wondering in confusion why the goblin was still standing there; alive but silent.

Then Shyola grinned and her soft voice drifted over to him. "I have this one under my spell."

Vexx stood fully upright, staring at the cave entrance. He thought he half-heard something from within, but it could just as easily have been the wind. *It doesn't seem like the other goblins noticed,* he thought, the seed of an idea sprouting in his mind as Shyola and her possessed goblin approached.

Vexx bent down, dispelling the ice from the dead goblin, and concentrated as he raised a hand above its frozen face and fed magic downward. The corpse of the goblin twitched—and then two glowing green eyes opened.

58

LERGU AND CHOC-KHRA

Shy and Vexx stood at the entrance of the cave, doing their best to see what was within. It seemed to go on for quite a long distance, though at some points, small, crudely shaped candles flickered in hollow alcoves on the sides.

"I suppose Kaylin was right," Shy said after a moment in a hushed voice. "This really *is* a big cave."

Vexx raised a finger to his lips. "Our voices could echo," he whispered. Shy nodded. "Let's send our goblins in first," he said, lighting their two torches with a gentle flame and setting them into both of the creatures' hands. "We'll sneak in behind them."

"A decent plan. I'll have mine do the talking," Shy said.

"Really? You can do that?"

Shy simply smirked and crept into the cave. Vexx glanced at his goblin, the undead creature staring back blankly. For a corpse, he looked fresh as ever, which didn't mean much by goblin standards. *Still, I doubt they'll notice he's undead…at first.*

At Vexx's mental urging, the undead goblin fell into a march alongside the possessed goblin, the torches of the two silent creatures lighting the way. Shy and Vexx walked a few paces behind, ready to hide or fight, should it come to that, ducking their heads down low when the passage narrowed and spreading out when it widened. They stepped past a giant stalactite and then shuffled closer together. When Shy's hand brushed Vexx's, she gave him a knowing wink.

The sound of a cheerful call broke the silence, followed by a few quick grunts. Vexx ducked down beside a stalactite, Shy cramming herself right next to him. Vexx peered over as their goblins approached another two, sheltering beside a stack of boxes, lanterns illuminating them. *Although it ruins their night vision,* Vexx thought with an accompanying mental eyeroll, breathing a bit easier. Though with the absence of imminent danger, it was growing increasingly difficult to not be distracted by the warm flesh pressed against his side.

The guards seemed to be asking their two goblins some questions in their own language. The goblin that Shy had possessed chattered back to them for a while.

"What's he saying?" Vexx asked, not expecting an answer, but surprisingly, Shyola seemed to be following along. *Perhaps all that time spent in various hells gives you the chance to learn different languages. Or perhaps she can just understand what her captured goblin can.*

"They're making a big fuss about Choc-Khra's glowing green eyes. They're wondering why he's not saying anything."

"Choc-Khra?" Vexx asked in confusion.

"Yes, that one is yours," Shyola replied. "Mine is

Lergu," she added, just as one of the guards snarled something.

"Lergu is explaining that Choc-Khra ate some strange mushroom and he's feeling unwell. But…"

"The game's up," Vexx snapped. "Let's attack."

Kill him, Vexx thought, sending the telepathic message to Choc-Khra. The undead goblin lurched forward, stabbing the guard, and an instant later, Lergu struck as well. Vexx and Shy stormed forward, but the only two goblins in the room were bleeding out on the ground, one of them groaning piteously in confusion. Shy stepped forward and smashed her heel into the goblin's skull.

Shy grinned over at Vexx, who was openly staring at her well-toned leg. "What next, Master?"

A scream sounded in the distance and wrenched Vexx away from his daydreams. Though it echoed from below, he had the sense that it wasn't far off. He scanned the room and took stock of what he had to work with. A few scattered boxes worth looting, several unfamiliar bones, and a canister of some liquid was hidden nearby in an alcove of glowing candles. Vexx stepped over, grabbed the canister and uncorked it before giving it a quick sniff.

Oil.

"I've got an idea," he said, turning to see where Shy was, who nodded down at the bodies.

"Do you want to raise them up? That might even the odds."

"No time," Vexx said, wiping the sweat off his brow. "Besides, I'm not sure I have the energy for it, and I'm all out of potions. Send your guy in first."

"And…do what?"

"I don't know, have him talk? Stall! They could be torturing Kaylin for all we know," Vexx said. "But first…"

The goblin had a leather bandolier that circled behind him, a strap that held his two-handed battle axe, and Vexx wedged the canister of oil between the leather and the tattered clothing of the possessed goblin.

"Perfect," Vexx muttered, clapping the goblin on the shoulder. "Send him in."

Lergu began shambling forward and Vexx crept through the shadows behind him, Shy pressed in close enough that he could feel her warm breath on his neck. The slope veered sharply to the left and sloped dangerously, the possessed goblin slid every few steps, and the two dungeoneers stepped carefully as they stuck close by. Vexx took a few steps forward, then froze as he heard Kaylin scream once again.

"Ah, such sweet agony," Shy whispered into Vexx's ear. Before he could respond, they heard the barking of goblin voices up ahead. Vexx leaned over to see their possessed goblin making his way into an open cavern ahead, which glowed brightly with light. There must have been a number of goblins inside—and Kaylin as well, likely tied up somewhere—but Vexx could only risk scattered glimpses.

"Have your goblin gather the others," Vexx hissed. "Then we can sneak up, protect Kaylin, and—"

"Just fireball the room!" Shy snapped, pointing forward. "Look! They're all clustered together! Lergu is rambling about this purple sheep he saw, and they seem sort of interested, but they're going to drift off in a moment."

Vexx took in a deep breath. Aside from the fact that he felt dangerously close to exhaustion, an uncontrolled explosion could put Kaylin in danger too. In the distance, he saw shapes closing in on Lergu and heard the distinct sounds of goblin chatter. *There's just no other choice. Even if I collapse, I have to strike now. We can only hope that Shy can pick off the rest.* He nodded and concentrated, spinning a molten ball of fire in his palm. He concentrated and ignored the sweat beading on his forehead and watched as his flame was joined by another and another as he gathered as much power as he could fit in the weaving circle of flames.

The Scorching Missile. I'd better not miss this one.

Vexx stormed down the passageway, sprinting closer and closer. Shy was right behind him. The first goblin to notice let out a short bark, then another glanced over, and Vexx readied himself. The metal of the canister of oil gleamed in the light as Vexx set his sights directly on Lergu, who was still standing in the middle.

Sorry, buddy, he thought as he dropped to one knee and fired his Scorching Missile directly into the fray.

The cavern exploded in a massive boom as the Scorching Missile burst into the canister of oil and blasted the entire gathering of goblins with flames. Vexx felt a wave of heat emanate from the chamber within as he panted for breath. Finally, it faded away, only to be replaced by the chuckling of Shyola as she strode past him. Vexx wiped his brow and lurched up to his feet.

"I do like my meat a little crispy," Shy called out. "Still alive, elf?"

59

BURNING GOBLINS

Vexx staggered against a wall and looked around frantically. "Kaylin? Kaylin, are you alright?" He waved away smoke and grimaced at the distinct smells of goblin and burning flesh. It was quite the bracing aroma, enough to cause more than a bit of nausea.

A burst of elven cursing brought Vexx's attention to a dusty bundle beside a cracked stalactite. The bundle moved slightly, and Vexx rushed over.

Kaylin, coated in dust and debris, shook her head and whirled on him. "Dammit, Vexx! You just about killed me!"

"It was Shy's idea," Vexx said, noticing the straps that still tied her to the stalactite. He flipped his knife open and cut the first strap away. "Anyway, we saved you. Just hold still…" Vexx slashed the last of the straps, and Kaylin groaned as she clambered to her feet.

"You just about burned my clothes off!" she complained, brushing off her tattered leather clothes. Small pebbles and bits of dirt fell to the ground, and more than a little ruined leather joined them. Vexx found himself staring dumbly as Kaylin brushed her chest off and he gulped as she turned around to shake rock fragments loose from her unbound hair. "How am I back there?" she called out, still shaking brushing herself off.

"Fine," Vexx choked out. "Very fine."

"Yeah, I guess it just caught me in the front," she said, turning back. "You owe me a new set of clothes after this, Vexx! I mean, look at me. I might as well not be wearing anything, these are barely hanging on." She glanced over at Shy, who had crossed her arms and was now glaring at the elf. "What?"

"Don't flirt with my Master."

"Well, you're not burnt at all," Vexx broke in. "The armor vendor was right, I guess. The less skin covered, the better the protection."

"Just with women, apparently," Kaylin grumbled. "You try running all day long with a stiff piece of leather wedged up your ass."

"I think I'll pass," Vexx said, wiping the sweat from his brow. Now that the fighting had come to an end, he felt his energy slowly recovering, and breathed out nice and easy. He had gotten used to this feeling from years of intense magical studies at the Academy, and he stood tall as he looked over the cavern. A bit of the remaining lantern oil and goblin carcasses were enough to keep a steady fire going, and the flickering light casted long shadows over the walls.

Something glinted and caught Vexx's eye. *Could that be?* He strode over, ignoring Shyola and Kaylin as they bickered about something or other. His eyes roved over the collection of charred leather satchels. He peered over, seeing some material poking out, blackened but with a hint of...gold!

"They're here!" he said, grabbing the first satchel and grinning as he looked within. The church's artifacts, perhaps a little worse for wear, but here nonetheless. Vexx whistled as the other dungeoneers approached. "It can't have been easy to drag these all the way up here." His smile faded. "Getting them down won't be too easy, either…"

Shy scoffed. "You youngsters make too big a deal of the little things. We're all done here, the goblins are dead, and all we have to do is take a nice walk back!" The succubus bent down, grabbed the straps of one satchel, and hefted it up on her shoulder. She grimaced. "It's not light, exactly, but…let's just turn this quest in and get our reward."

"The old lady is right," Kaylin added, grabbing another satchel. "Let's get this over with."

"Old lady?" Shy snarled as Vexx picked up the last one. "Why, I'll show you—"

"Let's go!" Vexx put a hand on each of their shoulders and insistently ushered them out of the cave.

60

THE PALADIN

"I can't believe those goblins were tickling me," Kaylin grumbled, trying to hold the remnants of her clothing together as the first rays of dawn lit the Lifeless Hills. "I'm very ticklish!"

"Huh," Vexx commented, too tired to do much thinking, every step made the heavy straps of the satchel cut painfully into his shoulders. *Gods above and below, once we're done with this, I could sleep for a day. With 100 gold coins, I could spring for a stay at an inn. A nice roast lamb, perhaps, with mashed potatoes. A mug of ale, or even a bucket of the stuff, and for dessert—*

"What's that over there?" Kaylin asked.

Vexx looked over and squinted. Something seemed to flash in the distance; a reflection caught by the morning light. After a moment, he saw movement, a knight in gleaming platemail and another figure in a dingy brown robe behind him, clambering their way up through the Lifeless Hills.

"Who cares," Vexx said. "It has nothing to do with us."

"They've spotted us," Kaylin said a moment later. "It seems they've changed their course a bit to meet us."

Vexx shrugged, but he felt a rising sense of danger as he looked below, watching the two strangers moving over to meet them. *They look pretty experienced to me...at least, the knight is. Much more experienced than us, like he's on an entirely different level. You can't get platemail like that for cheap, and he seems strong enough to wear it without any problem.*

Shy sniffed. "Those two positively reek of righteous fervor. Master, I...I would advise caution."

Vexx gritted his teeth. *They're heading straight toward us, but why?*

"Hey, you down there!" Vexx shouted. "Where are you headed?"

The knight paused, his helmet shimmering in the light as he looked up. There were two massive wings on both ends with blue decorations. After a moment, he took the helmet off and glared at the party of tired dungeoneers.

"Those are the holy relics of Cloudbury in your satchels, or am I wrong? Do not think to deceive me."

"They are...but we have reclaimed them. The quest was posted in Cloudbury, and we accepted the bounty."

The paladin scoffed. "Nonsense. I see you there, demon, baring all your flesh and corrupting those who look upon you. Consorting with an elf and a warlock? I care not to think how you've already befouled these holy relics."

Vexx spread his arms out wide. "I think we have a misunderstanding here. You see—"

"Know now, you lost, foul souls," the paladin proclaimed, "That it is I, the Holy Knight Mantaneal Thurmon, the legendary paladin and demon slayer, who sends you to your hells. My faithful servant and I have come to exact vengeance on you heretics for stealing the sacred relics of Cloudbury. You should know this before you are vanquished," he concluded, setting his heavy helmet back on his head.

61

A GIANT MISUNDERSTANDING

"Mantaneal Thurmon?" Kaylin repeated slowly as the paladin trudged up the hill, the cleric hurrying along beside him.

"Mantaneal…" Vexx sounded out, furrowing his brow. "Oh yes, I've heard of him! He went monster hunting a few times with Dred Wyrm!"

"I don't know who either of those two are, darling, but I do think you two should begin firing while we have the advantage," Shyola pointed out, materializing her glowing orange whip and readying herself.

"Oh, no." Vexx smiled. "This has all been just a giant misunderstanding. You see, we were actually—"

The cleric raised his staff in the air, the crystal at the top glowed brightly with energy, and a wave of sparkling magic circled around the paladin. He seemed to move a half-step faster, raising his sword up high, a solid shield guarding his left side.

"Accept your deaths!"

"They mean it, Vexx!" Kaylin cried in alarm, loosing

an arrow at Sir Thurmon. The holy knight raised his shield almost contemptuously, catching it on his oaken crest.

Vexx cursed, but sprang into action, firing a gout of flames into the grass and rock just ahead of Sir Thurmon. The flames rose, a wall of fire blocking the paladin's path, and Vexx took a deep breath.

"Like I was saying, your quarrel is not with us!"

A dark figure emerged behind the flames, then strode straight through, a shimmering magical shield flickered a myriad of colors as it struggled to protect the paladin. Sir Thurmon slowed, then continued his unstoppable march forward. "My quarrel," he boomed out, echoing from behind his helmet, "is with enemies of the church. Such as you!"

Another arrow soared out, this one impaling itself in a small gap in the gleaming armor, but it barely seemed to affect the paladin as he strode forward.

"Fuck!" Vexx snapped, glancing down at the cleric, still keeping some distance away as he chanted. "Kaylin, keep this guy busy!" he said, dashing to the side.

"Wh—what?" the elf replied, stumbling back a step as she tried to put more distance between her and the paladin. "Uh, how?"

"Just keep shooting! Shy, with me! Let's kill the cleric."

"Ooh, you're speaking my language," Shy purred as she sprinted down the cliffside. Vexx struggled to keep up and kept an eye on Kaylin as she squealed and backed away from the approaching paladin. *We'll be back for you soon. Don't die now!*

Vexx gritted his teeth and summoned a fireball around his fist. He punched forward, the fireball sailing down to the cleric, who spun his staff in an attempt to deflect the fireball. It slammed into him, but disappeared as he whirled his magic staff, leaving scorch marks on his brown robe. The cleric staggered back a pace or two. He coughed, then slammed the staff into the ground, reaching for something in his satchel.

Shy lunged and struck, her orange whip slicing through the air and rending the cleric clean in half just as he raised his fist in the air. The cleric's eyes widened, his mouth half open—and then the top and bottom halves of the dead man dropped to the ground with a sickening thud.

Shyola grinned over. "He's not so tough."

"Vexx!" Kaylin shouted, farther uphill.

"We're coming!" Vexx shouted back, sinking down, his hands on his knees as he breathed in and out. He was exhausted. *What I wouldn't give for a potion right now.* "Just…just hold him off!"

"No, Vexx!" she shouted, and he heard the sharp clank of an arrow glancing off of platemail not very far away. "He's coming for you!"

Vexx and Shyola turned, and to their combined horror, they saw the paladin barreling down towards them. "Brother Bernard!" he screamed. "Noooo!"

62

THE VERGE OF DEATH

"Fuck," was all Vexx could manage as the paladin charged at him, his sword upraised in an underhand grip, the single moment stretching into an eternity. Vexx fired a rushed fireball at the charging knight and was rewarded with a grunt—and then Vexx screamed as pain lanced through him. His eyes dropped to his stomach and he stared dumbly at the protruding hilt of the paladin's sword, the blade buried deep in his abdomen.

"Don't kill my Master, dickbag!" Shyola shouted, and then Vexx dimly heard the snapping of her whip. The helmet looked left and then a plated boot planted itself on Vexx's chest and the paladin forced his sword free.

Vexx collapsed to the ground and couldn't stop himself from rolling a short distance down the hill. He rolled a couple times before getting wedged somewhere, finally motionless. Vexx gritted his teeth and clenched both hands to the spreading wetness in his stomach, gasping as he felt for the jagged hole the longsword had left inside him.

This... Vexx raised his left hand up, his glove drenched

in dripping blood, his vision flickering. *Is this what death feels like?* He groaned, looking to his side, trying to block out the pain as he took stock of his surroundings. There was a dim clatter of fighting, and then a spinning arrow sailing past, as if it had been deflected. But around him…

Vexx felt the peculiar softness of the ground around him, and realized he was lying beside the corpse of Brother Bernard. *Or part of him. Fitting, I suppose.* But Vexx summoned a last burst of strength, half-turning and gripping the dead cleric's leather satchel with his two blood-soaked gloves.

I'm not dying yet. Fuck that!

He groped around desperately for the leather satchel, fumbling it open when he finally had it in his grasp. He didn't dare hope as he heard the familiar clanking of glass vials within it. Vexx stuck his left hand in and grabbed several potions. As he pulled them out of the satchel, his vision swam and he squinted, trying to make sense of the potions. Vexx felt his pulse slow and his energy seemed to slip away.

That…that one's red!

He gripped the potion with the last of his strength, bloodying it as his fingers slipped over the slick glass. Fighting the panic and desperation, he gripped the cork, his fumbling fingers feeling like lead and he struggled to raise it to his lips. Vexx gritted his teeth and wrenched it open before greedily pouring it into his mouth, drinking it up, gurgling weakly as the potent mixture made its way inside him. His agony intensified as the magic worked within him.

Drained in a moment, the last thing Vexx remembered was watching the vial slip out of his hand and hearing the distant sound of glass as it shattered on the rocks below.

63

FIGHTING TOGETHER

The sounds seemed to come from a great distance. The grunt of a man's voice, as if recoiling from an impact. The steady thrum of a bow. The snap of a whip.

"Vexx..."

My mother's voice? I haven't heard her voice in years, not since the plague that took her.

"Vexx, my boy!"

Father's voice! Vexx grinned weakly, but his smile quickly faded. *He'll be so disappointed that I got expelled. And after all their sacrifices...*he coughed, rolling over to one side, his hand falling to where the longsword had impaled him. His robe was wet, though the wound had somehow closed itself up. Vexx groaned as he felt a wave of nausea wash over him.

"Watch out, Shy!"

Slowly, Vexx's foggy head cleared, and he heard the shouts and clatter of the fight uphill. He glanced upward as he staggered to his knees. *They need my help. But first...* Vexx grabbed the dead cleric's remaining potions and took stock of the few different potions before taking a big gulp of a swirling blue fluid. He felt a rush of energy around him and put his palm just above the dead cleric's head.

You won't be too helpful now, but every bit counts, Vexx thought as he cast his necromantic energy downward. The cleric's eyes shot open, the glowing green orbs a welcome sight. Vexx got to his feet, already summoning the energy for a fireball, watching as Shy desperately darted away from the paladin's swing. Kaylin loosed an arrow behind him, sticking into the man's back, but the paladin continued pursuing the succubus.

"Over here, you asshole!" Vexx shouted as he fired a fireball at him. The blast exploded on the paladin's sturdy left pauldron, knocking him off balance for a moment and buying Shyola the time to dart away, but still, the paladin advanced as calmly as ever. But their efforts were rewarded: his armor was scorched, a few arrows stuck up out of him, and fresh cuts on his armor showed where Shy's whip had left its marks.

He could butcher each one of us in a one-on-one fight. But together? We still have a chance.

Vexx put another heavy burst of magic into the Scorching Missile that he sent flying over to the paladin. It streamed forward in a reddish orange haze, bursting on the paladin's armor. The paladin stopped this time, roaring in pain and rage, waving away the spreading flames on his armor. Shy leaped forward and slammed her whip into the paladin's unguarded side, and Kaylin cheered as the paladin rolled down the hill. His armor clanked and clattered as he rolled end over end a half dozen times.

Then, Sir Thurmon's armored hand grasped a stray branch, the slim branch somehow enough to hold him in place. He clambered to his feet, brushing away the last smoldering embers, and looked over at Vexx.

"Just give up," the paladin boomed from behind his helmet. He paused, fumbling for his satchel, and his plated hand brought out a gigantic jug of red health potion. He raised it up to his helmet, tilting his head back and then—

An arrow sailed toward it, buffeted to the side by the wind, but curving an instant later and taking the jug square in the center. Glass shattered everywhere, red liquid splashing against the paladin's helmet and platemail.

"Hey!" the paladin shouted. "You asshole! Who does that?"

"He's weak," Shy called out as the paladin reached down into his satchel again. "It's now or never! Hit him with everything you've got!"

As if snapping out of a trance, Vexx stepped forward, his two hands extended. He punched forward, left then right, sending blistering fireball after fireball. The paladin staggered back, his shield taking part of the blow, but his footing wasn't secure here. Rocks clattered from uphill, and Vexx glanced up as his energy drained, seeing Kaylin and Shyola rushing down.

"I'll snare him," Kaylin shouted as they ran. "Keep him busy, Shy!"

"You got it," she replied, slashing her whip downward. Sir Thurmon jerked his head to the side, and the whip severed one of his helmet's decorative wings. He tossed his charred and smoldering shield to the ground, grabbing his battered longsword with both hands. He stepped aside, somehow dodging another one of Vexx's fireballs, even as he parried Shy's whip with his sword. Sir Thurmon's left hand shot out toward Vexx as he readied another fireball.

"Paralyze!" the paladin shouted, and in an instant, Vexx froze in place. Then the paladin barreled forward, harrying the succubus, drawing blood with a quick stab. Two quick slashes and he was on her, sword raised high. "Begone, foul dem—gah!"

Kaylin had snared him with her trap, the net circled around the single remaining wing of his helmet, and she jerked it back as he struggled against it. The helmet slid up, and then Sir Thurmon pushed it off, whirling around and catching it. Instead of letting go, he pulled back on the rope, grabbing and dragging Kaylin forward. She reeled back and stumbled down the sloping hill just as the paladin's wild swing cut through where she had been.

64

PARALYZED

"K ay...inn!" Vexx choked out, straining against the paralyzing spell. He could wiggle his toes now, though that was little relief, as the red-faced paladin strode to the elf as she stumbled away. With his unkept blond hair and splotchy face, he looked like an annoyed logger under all of that shiny armor. Vexx's fingers twitched, and he felt a bit more sensation in his body.

Just a bit more...

"Come here, you," the paladin rasped as he pulled her in, the scene strangely reminiscent of a fisherman reeling in a fish. "Get over he—"

A flashing whip scythed through the net trap and sent the paladin and the elf staggering back, the wounded Shyola glaring as she slashed her whip back. The paladin lurched forward, stopping only to parry the whip aside and then continued his attack on Kaylin.

"By all the saints," Sir Thurmon huffed, "you're an annoying bunch. Just...give...up!" he shouted, swinging his sword up above Kaylin.

Shyola prowled close, knocking the blade away with a

powerful slash, then turned to Kaylin. "Get out of here, elf!" she yelled, slapping Kaylin's butt with an empowered spank and launching her in the air to fall a dozen paces away. Sir Thurmun slammed her in the chest with the pommel of his sword, driving her back, then with another wild swing, he sent the succubus tumbling down the hill.

Groaning, the paladin turned, just as Vexx flexed one hand and then the other. *The spell is wearing off!* The paladin looked a mess, his armor chipped and askew, and part of it was burnt away to reveal angry, red skin underneath. He looked flustered, blood dripping from Sir Thurmon's broken nose, and his angry red face latched itself onto Vexx. The paladin took one step forward, then another.

Fucking hells! How much does it take to kill this guy?

"You! This is all your fault," Sir Mantaneal Thurmon spat, baring his teeth and stomping forward as Vexx tried desperately to form a fireball in his half-frozen hand. *Come on, come on, almost there!* A faint spark appeared in front of Vexx's extended hand. "It's your fault Brother Bernard—"

The paladin lunged forward and inexplicably tripped, falling in a crash of metal. Slowly, he looked back. The undead corpse of Brother Bernard—the top half, anyway —had grasped him firmly by the ankle.

"Unhand me, Brother!" the paladin roared, turning back and chopping off the hand with a heavy swing. Then Vexx breathed in, summoning all his energy reserves, and fired a full blast of flames right into Sir Thurmon's exposed face. The gout of fire mercifully blocked out Vexx's vision as the spray of flames continued, licking at the paladin's platemail and charring it, the armor at the top glowing orange as if at a blacksmith's forge—and then it faded away, Vexx's energy was completely spent. He gasped and would have collapsed if the paralyzing spell had faded away entirely, but as it was, he just hung limply in the air.

Sir Thurmon wasn't so lucky.

The paladin dropped to the ground, a smoking ruin where his head had been, trails of smoke rising through the gaps in his armor as if it was a makeshift oven. The orange glow around his neck slowly faded away, even as it continued smoldering. The sounds of loose rock and dirt sliding away announced the return of Shyola and Kaylin. Vexx craned his neck to look up at them.

They look worse for wear. We all do. Vexx's eyes flicked down to the dead paladin. *But it could be worse.*

Suddenly, the paralyzing spell faded away, and Vexx dropped groaning to the ground. He pushed himself up to see Shyola reaching a hand down. In silence, Vexx gripped the outstretched hand, and she hauled him to his feet. Kaylin approached, gingerly rubbing her butt.

"My ass is still red," Kaylin complained. "I think you left a mark."

"Well, I saved that ass of yours," Shy pointed out.

"Thanks."

"You're welcome."

The moment lingered. *It's not much, but at least they're working together.* After a second, Vexx realized he should break the silence, and he coughed. "So…should we loot the body?"

65

ALL DOWNHILL FROM HERE

Vexx hefted the huge sword, wincing at the thought of lugging that all the way back, much less fighting with it. *That paladin must have been unbelievably strong.* He looked over at Shyola and frowned, dropping the weapon.

"That's not looting, Shy. That's disrespectful."

"What?" Shy dropped the tunic she was peeking under. "I was just curious. Some of these chaste sorts, well, you can understand why, but—"

"Enough."

"Yeah, I'd say it is."

Vexx shook his head, moving on to the cleric, keeping his footing despite his exhaustion. He gave the lower half of Brother Bernard a cursory once-over. He'd already rummaged through it before, but that had been a matter of life and death. He took the time to investigate now, finding little else beside a few herbs, a half-eaten loaf of bread, and a couple holy trinkets that might fetch a few coppers.

Just when he was about done, he looked over to see a

rolled up scroll tightly clenched in the cleric's left hand. Vexx uncurled the cleric's stiff fingers and pried the scroll loose. He wasn't expecting much, but paused as he read the title.

Spell for Banishing Demons to the Lower Realms.

Banishing a demon! The cleric was about to cast this when Shy killed him. Would it have worked?

Vexx cast a furtive glance at Shyola.

This could come in handy. He hated himself for the thought, but stuffed it into his pocket all the same. *I can't trust her, for sure. They seem to be getting along now, but what if we fall into the worst case scenario? If Shyola tries to drain Kaylin's soul again?*

Vexx bit his lip. *I'm not sure exactly what I'd do, but at least I have the option now.*

"Find anything?"

"Nothing," he replied hoarsely, then coughed. "S'cuse me. Nothing besides a few trinkets and a couple potions."

Kaylin emerged from down the slope, a few arrows in her hand, and she raised them in the air in triumph. "I can use some of these again!"

"That's great," Vexx replied, moving back up to the paladin's corpse. Shy prodded the sword with her heel.

"I don't much like the idea of bringing that back," the succubus said.

"Me neither."

Vexx stared down at the lifeless body of the paladin, unsure even where to start. *Well, it worked with the cleric, and he'd been cut clean in half.* He put his palm just about the paladin's chest armor, closing his eyes in concentration, sending a surge of magical energy downward. He opened his eyes.

The body was silent for a moment. Then it twitched, a

groaning rumble forming, one elbow dug into the ground as it struggled to rise to its feet. Vexx leaned forward, helping support the undead paladin as it clambered to its feet. *Strange that I'm helping it now, after all that fighting.* He stepped back a pace.

"What are you doing, Vexx?" Kaylin asked, a satchel on one shoulder. "Let's get out of these damn hills already."

"I don't know about you," Vexx said, stepping back carefully as the undead paladin rose to his feet, almost falling over. "But I'm not carrying any more than I have to. Let's use him as a pack mule for a while. Besides, the melt value on his armor alone has to be worth a pretty penny."

"Good thinking, Master," Shyola called out, hauling her satchel over. "Hey, zombie. Stand still, will you?"

The paladin shifted impatiently as Shyola carefully strapped her satchel full of gold artifacts onto its back. She grinned, grabbed Vexx's bag and added it to the weight. The zombie let out a low grumble. Kaylin approached, eagerly holding the satchel in her arms.

"Yeah, this will make it much eas—"

Kaylin slid on some loose pebbles and stumbled forward before awkwardly sprawling into the armored zombie. The undead paladin simply grunted, barely rocking at all, and Kaylin looked up sheepishly.

"Heh…whoops."

"Stop playing around and get it loaded," Shy snapped, helping Kaylin attach the last satchel.

Vexx nodded in satisfaction. He still felt drained from that fight and from wandering around the Lifeless Hills for hours. "Zombie Thurmon, lead the way back to Cloudbury!"

The paladin took one confident step forward into empty air, then lurched forward, falling all the way down the rest of the hill, clattering and rolling noisily until the body slid into a tree at the bottom.

Vexx gritted his teeth. "Well, he has the right idea, anyway. Let's go, you two. It's just through the forest and as long as he doesn't bump into any trees, we'll be just fine."

66

ACT NATURAL

Vexx winced at the sound of branches scraping against metal as the undead paladin staggered past yet another tree.

"That is not a pleasant sound," Shyola remarked as she stuck her fingers in her ears. "Let me steer this thing. It needs to stop bumping into trees."

"Don't touch... me..." the undead paladin rasped, jerking its gauntlet away as Shyola reached for it. "De... mon..."

"Well, that's rude," Shyola said. "I'm just trying to—"

"Shush!" Kaylin snapped, her ears twitching.

"That's *also* rude," Shyola grumbled.

"There's a party of loggers coming down the road," Kaylin explained. "They're going to see that his head is all...gone."

Vexx fumbled with the paladin's damaged helmet and hurried over, hastily putting it on the paladin's neck. "Just act natural," Vexx muttered through gritted teeth.

Shyola snorted. "How natural do you expect a half-naked elf, a necromancer, a succubus, and the reanimated corpse of a paladin to act?"

"More natural than you're acting!"

The dungeoneers clenched their teeth and waved at the passing party of bemused loggers. They walked a few paces forward, and then a moment later, the paladin's helmet toppled off his moving body. Vexx scrambled to pick it back up and place it back on the dead paladin's head.

"Shit, do you think they saw?" he hissed.

"No," Kaylin said, glancing back.

"We can't keep doing this," Shy said. "We're almost at Cloudbury by now."

"It just...it won't stay on," Vexx grumbled, trying to get the ruined helmet to stay in place. "It's so much harder when he doesn't have a head!"

"This isn't going to work anymore," Shy insisted. "We'll have to carry the rest on foot. Or maybe leave him here."

"But the melt value of the armor alone!" Vexx grumbled, then widened his eyes. "Oh, I just thought of something! Brother Bernard had an unopened strength potion. I'll pass it around as a bit of a pick-me-up. Take a swig each and it should last us to the reliquary."

"Fine," Kaylin said. "But I'm drinking first. I don't know where Shy's mouth has been," she said, taking a sip and handing it over to Vexx, who drank another third.

"Oh, so many places," Shy purred and took the potion. "Bottoms up," she said, putting the potion between her lips and jerking her head back. She tapped the end of the potion and then pulled it out, winking at Vexx. "I like to make sure I swallow everything."

"Great, great," Vexx muttered, feeling vaguely uncomfortable, stuck between Kaylin's disapproving stare and Shy's sly smirk. "Let's just turn this quest in already."

"Hmm, why don't you two support the paladin on the way in. As for me, Master," Shyola said as she hefted the bag of relics, "I'm more than willing to take your big load on my back."

67

THE MELT VALUE ALONE

"That's right," the priest was saying to the growing crowd, and judging by their assortment of weapons and armor, they were an adventurous bunch. "Quite a lot of relics, and we suspect they headed in the direction of the Lifeless Hills. 100 coins are in it for you if you bring… back…" Gaius trailed off, now noticing the approach of the dungeoneers, the paladin supported between them. "What is the meaning of this? Why have you come back?"

"Got your relics," Vexx wheezed, struggling to catch his breath as the crowd grumbled in annoyance. A line formed for them as the crowd began dispersing, disappointed would-be adventurers already leaving the square, now that the quest had been completed by someone else.

"I told you not to come back here," Gaius grumbled. "Who…" he blinked. "Is that…"

"The holy knight, Mantaneal Thurmon. Apparently he'd been killed, along with a cleric, but I thought it best to bring him back here. He was a renowned paladin, you know, and I thought…a stately burial here…" Vexx tapped the platemail. "And the melt value alone...well, what I mean is, we're charging extra for the corpse."

The priest frowned. The square outside the reliquary had just about cleared away by now, the last of the dungeoneers leaving to find new quests. "That isn't very... pious of you."

"I leave piety to prophets, and profit-less piety is poverty. Just think about it!" Vexx said. "Here rests the brave Sir Thurmon, legendary paladin. Felled by goblins while on a holy quest. Think of the pilgrims! Think of the tithes you'd get from visitors!"

"Hmm..." Gaius nodded. "Alright. Three gold coins."

"What? Ten, at least. The melt value of the armor alone—"

"Melt value!" the priest sniffed in disdain. "What are you, a dwarf? Five, and we keep the armor. A holy knight should be buried in his armor. It's only fitting."

Vexx grimaced, then let the paladin clatter to the ground. "Fine," he said, rubbing his shoulder. "I'm through with carrying him."

"I still can't believe you hauled him all the way down from the Lifeless Hills," the priest said. "And you, a scrawny kid."

"I'm stronger than I look," Vexx muttered.

"Sure you are," Gaius sniffed. "No doubt you're half-doped up on strength potion. And you, foul creature," the priest added as Shyola approached with her overloaded bag.

"Here are your decorations," the succubus replied, setting the heavy load on the ground. "I'm a succubus, darling, I can handle a big package."

The priest barged forward with a wide smile, the dungeoneers making space for him, and he spread open the bag and looked inside. The smile dropped in an instant.

"What!? These are scorched! How could you let this happen!?"

"They're not that scorched," Vexx protested as the priest raised a few burned golden items in the air, checking them over carefully before setting them aside. The priest shot Vexx a glare.

"What happened?"

"Look, I don't know," Vexx said, spreading his arms out wide. "I couldn't tell you what the goblins were up to. I was just…I was just healing people. I had nothing to do with any of that."

"Ruined," Gaius muttered, setting more of the artifacts to the side. The normally gleaming gold artifacts were charred either black or a dull copper.

"They're not," Vexx said, creating a small ball of ice at his fingertips and grabbing a large golden scepter. He rubbed the ice against it, getting a bit of the black flakes off. "Look, it just needs a bit of polishing. That's all. Can we take our 100 coins now?"

"No, I'm only giving you half. Some of these parchments are burned to a crisp. The holy spear of Farnarius is just a blackened stick with a bit of metal at the end."

"Well…you could say he killed a dragon with it."

"I don't need your marketing advice."

"Half?" Vexx muttered, glancing at the other dungeoneers. He was rewarded with shrugs. *I guess the priest has a point.* "Fifty-five coins, counting the paladin."

"Fine," Gaius said, setting the last artifact down. He extended his hand, though his scowl remained. They shook on it, the priest exerting more pressure than was polite, but Vexx used his boosted strength to squeeze right back. The priest's eye twitched, and he retracted his hand. "I'll get your money."

"We're *so* happy to work with you," Vexx piped up cheerfully.

I think it's about time we got out of town.

68

THE QUEST COMPLETED

They waited in silence as the priest left, Vexx slowly feeling his surge of strength fading away and being replaced by exhaustion. "I'll need a drink after this."

"At least we can afford it," Kaylin said cheerily. "Right, Vexx?"

"Right."

"Some new clothes too," Kaylin said, examining the tattered leather that still somehow clung to her body. "This is just a mess. Still, I look nicer than Shyola," she added with a smirk.

Shyola frowned. "That is absolutely absurd! You! *You?*" She snorted. "Oh, there's a certain trashy attraction some lower classes of species might have to you," Shy said. "Which brings me to the idea of a potentially profitable money making enterprise. Listen to this, Master. Just imagine, a somewhat innocent woman wandering the road in those rags, just begging for some horny bandits to ambush you? Then, Master, we could spring out of hiding to loot the corpses and—"

"Would Kaylin be one of the corpses?"

Shyola paused to consider. She shrugged. "I don't know exactly how it would play out. I'm a succubus, darling, not a prophetess. But, Master, I think we should seriously consider—"

Kaylin snorted and stomped away. After a few moments, she came up to Vexx, a scowl on her face. "Vexx, normally I'd say we split it fifty-fifty-fifty, but with Shyola, I think we should only give her a third," Kaylin whispered to Vexx.

"Right. I was thinking the same thing," he replied, and Kaylin grinned, putting a finger to her lips.

Vexx turned back to see the tall priest emerge from the door with a heavy sack of coins, several servants trailing along with him to collect the satchels laden with the golden artifacts.

"Here it is!" Gaius snapped, "You know," he added with a scowl. "I'm growing skeptical of your story about Sir Thurmon. A handful of goblins overpowered him? Sir Thurmon, one of the most legendary dungeoneers in the land?"

"That's right. Where he failed, Vexx White succeeded. Remember the name, priest."

The priest sneered. "He must have killed most of the goblins first. I just don't know what to make of this."

"So what are you saying?" Vexx snapped, leaning forward inquisitively. "Do you really think *we* could have killed him?"

Gaius scoffed. "Of course not."

"So there you have it!"

The priest grunted, tossing the sack of gold coins on the ground. "Now begone, you...*witches*."

"Until next time."

"No! There will be no next time."

"Well…" Vexx shrugged, counting the coins. "We'll see."

"We will not see. There simply will be no next time. Should you show up again, we will have you driven out and—"

"Looks like it's all here," Vexx said, satisfied with the fifty-five coins. "See you later!"

The dungeoneers turned around, clanking with their coins, smiling as they made their way to the tavern while the priest glared behind them.

"I got nothing for you," the barkeep said immediately as the dungeoneers approached the counter. "Look, you're capable enough, I'll give you that. I've already heard plenty of talk from more than a few pissed off adventurers on their way out of town."

"The poster board is empty outside, too," Vexx added.

"I heard people have been ripping the posters off to get rid of the competition." Pollander shook his head in sadness. "I don't know who would do such a thing! Well, at least everything's quiet now. It's nice and peaceful, aside from a bit of shady business with the logging companies... but I stay out of that nonsense."

"Yeah, nice and peaceful. Bit of a problem for us," Vexx said, "but right now, I just want that round of ale you promised."

"You remembered that," Pollander said, his eye twitching. "You know, I got to thinking, once I heard all the chatter about goblins stealing the holy artifacts. Seems you figured killing goblins would solve both problems."

"Was I wrong?"

"No," the barkeep said, filling up a mug. "You're a sneaky bastard, I'll give you that." He passed out the mugs to the dungeoneers, Kaylin opting to take one this time, and Vexx found them a table of their own. The elf and the succubus settled into their seats without comment, and for a moment, Vexx entertained the delusion that after all they had been through, the two were finally getting along.

"We've been doing well," Vexx began, grinning at the two of them. "They say nine out of ten dungeoneers die before their tenth quest. It's not an easy life, but we're living it."

"Have we done ten quests though?" Kaylin asked, leaning back in thought. "We've fought plenty, but as far as quests go…"

"Ah…I suppose not."

"Dungeoneer," Shyola mused beside Vexx. "That still takes some getting used to. I suppose it's entertaining enough, anyway. For now."

"A toast," Vexx said, raising his mug. "To new beginnings! You know, I felt I had fallen as low as I could ever get, coming back to Cloudbury. Kicked out of the Magical Academy at Fallanden, my father dead, no place to live… but you two have both taught me something."

Kaylin nodded. "There's never really a bottom. You can always keep falling. Unless," she said, gesturing with her mug, the froth dribbling off the edge. "There's a net to catch you. And trap you."

"Uh…yeah." Vexx blinked. "Anyway, I'm glad to have met you both. To our next adventures!"

They all raised a mug in salute. Vexx drank deeply, ignoring Kaylin as she coughed and sputtered.

Shyola set her mug down and tut-tutted. "Adventures are all well and good, but new beginnings mean cutting out old ties and starting afresh. I'm telling you, Master, that elf has to go. I want you all to myself! Besides, there's no point in keeping her around when there aren't any quests available!" Shy leaned in close. "You and me, let's take some time off. I can su—"

The tavern door slammed open, the few patrons left in the half-deserted building looked over as a farmer in a wide-brimmed hat staggered forward, pausing to rest his calloused hands on his knees and to take a few shuddering breaths. Then, he jerked his panicked eyes up.

"I need adventurers for a quest, and I need them *now!*"

ABOUT THE AUTHOR

You know those kids who live in the pale blue light of their computer monitors? Well, J. E. Thompson was one of those youngsters. His childhood was spent obsessing over warlocks and bonus points, tirelessly questing to defeat the threats in his crumbling virtual empires, and above all, creating worlds and adventures for himself and his friends to enjoy.

But that scrawny swashbuckler has long since grown up, and these days, instead of planning out Dungeons and Dragons campaigns, J. E. Thompson is a software developer who has worked for some of the industry's top players, like the legendary Rockstar Games.

As a fiction author, he has written a fantasy adventure series titled The White Chronicles, which follows a cocky human warlock with a penchant for trouble. When he isn't dreaming up new adventures, J. E. Thompson is enjoying a quiet life in South Carolina with his wife and poodle.

For more information:
jetwrites.com
hello@jetwrites.com
@jet_writes

THE ADVENTURE CONTINUES

CPSIA information can be obtained
at www.ICGtesting.com
Printed in the USA
FSHW011647280520
70528FS